MMXII

THE WHITE REVIEW

EDITORS   BENJAMIN EASTHAM & JACQUES TESTARD
DESIGN, ART DIRECTION   RAY O'MEARA
ASSISTANT EDITOR   MARY HANNITY
EDITORIAL ASSISTANTS   STEPHEN MCEWEN, OLIVER TAYLOR

POETRY EDITOR   J. S. TENNANT
ONLINE EDITOR   KISHANI WIDYARATNA
CONTRIBUTING EDITORS   JACOB BROMBERG, LAUREN ELKIN, EMMELINE FRANCIS,
                               LEE ROURKE, SAM SOLNICK

FUNDING & DEVELOPMENT   SOPHIE LEIGH-PEMBERTON
TRUSTEES   MICHAEL AMHERST, HANNAH BARRY, ANN & MICHAEL CAESAR,
                               BLAINE COOK, HUGUES DE DIVONNE, TOM MORRISON-BELL,
                               NIALL HOBHOUSE, CATARINA LEIGH-PEMBERTON, MICHAEL LEUE,
                               AMY POLLNER, PROFESSOR ANDREW PEACOCK,
                               CÉCILE DE ROCHEQUAIRIE, HUBERT TESTARD, MICHEL TESTARD,
                               DANIELA & RON WILLSON, CAROLINE YOUNGER,
HONORARY TRUSTEES   DEBORAH COX, WILLIAM MORGAN

COVER ART BY MATT CONNORS

PRINTED BY PUSH, LONDON
PAPER BY ANTALIS MCNAUGHTON (OLIN CREAM ROUGH 100GSM, OLIN HIGH WHITE 120GSM)
BESPOKE PAPER MARBLE BY PAYHEMBURY MARBLE PAPERS
TYPESET IN JOYOUS (BLANCHE)

PUBLISHED BY THE WHITE REVIEW, DECEMBER 2012
EDITION OF 1,000
ISBN No. 978-0-9568001-6-9

THE WHITE REVIEW, 1 KNIGHTSBRIDGE GREEN, LONDON SW1X 7QA
WWW.THEWHITEREVIEW.ORG

CONTENTS

CONTENTS

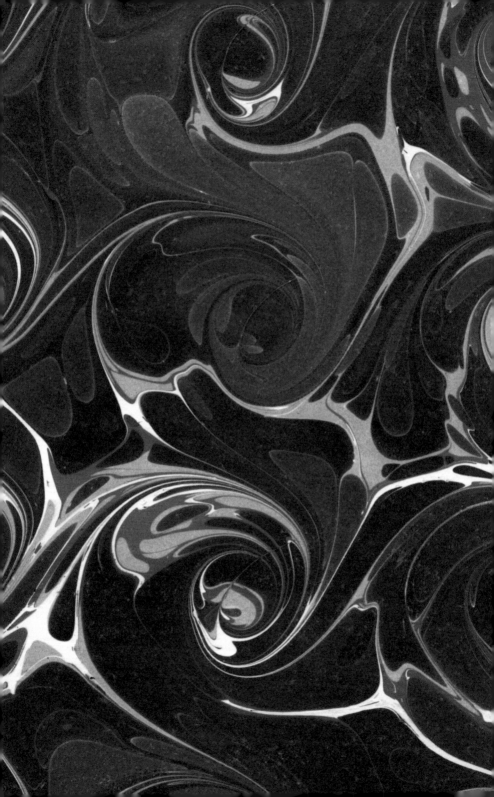

EDITORIAL

BY THE LOOKS OF IT, not much has changed for THE WHITE REVIEW. This new edition, like its predecessors, features the customary blend of interviews, fiction, essays, poetry and artwork, and gives pride of place to talented young writers such as Jack Cox, whose story 'The Fishermen' opens the issue. Subscribers will also notice that we have stuck to our tradition of stretching the calendrical boundaries of the quarterly publishing cycle.

So what is new? A sea change for THE WHITE REVIEW was the obtainment of charitable status late this summer. As a registered charity, we aim to promote 'the arts and literature for the benefit of the public by the publication of an arts and literary journal and the organisation of artistic and literary events specialising in artistically or educationally meritorious works of new or emerging artists and writers'.

What this means, in effect, is that we are eligible for gift-aid on all donations. We would also like to expand our charitable board of Trustees — currently a triumvirate, including both editors – in the hope that THE WHITE REVIEW can continue to flourish. In the meantime, as we figure out how to reclaim gift-aid (these things do not come easily to us), we have stepped tentatively into the realm of advertising as a way of part-funding our production costs. We are pleased to have secured the support of a small number of similarly-minded cultural organisations such as the Wellcome Trust in this endeavour.

The last – and most exciting – development, is the launch of a short story prize, imaginatively named THE WHITE REVIEW SHORT STORY PRIZE. Funded by a generous £2,500 grant from the Jerwood Charitable Foundation, all of which will be awarded to the winner, the prize is open to submissions until 1 March 2013. This competition, to be judged by writer Deborah Levy, editor Alex Bowler and literary agent Karolina Sutton, will reward the best story submitted to THE WHITE REVIEW by an unpublished writer residing in Great Britain or Ireland (do visit our website for details). Meanwhile, there is an issue to read. As ever, we hope it inspires, provokes, angers. Any reaction is a gratifying one.

THE EDITORS

THE FISHERMEN

BY

JACK COX

THE DAY HE ARRIVED in Rome Milan bought a newspaper for the classifieds and some oranges from a vendor at the train terminal whose eyes went from the money to the coat it came from in one doubtful curve. It was not a very cool morning but aside from the new things he tucked under his arm as he ran for a passing bus, everything that Milan owned was in his coat.

He got down from the bus before it crossed over the Tiber to Prati and followed a flight of marble steps to the riverbank. With the newspaper spread before him he circled openings for all kinds of work and if his pencil came down and stayed he took a dictionary from his pocket and propped it open on his knee. He peeled an orange with his free hand, threw the skin on the garbage caught between the rocks beneath his feet and spat the pips into the river.

As the day got warmer he made a pillow with the coat and stretched out on the stone. The slow white clouds throbbed in his eyes. He was tired after the hours spent cooped in the trains and was beginning to drift asleep when two boys came scampering over the rocks with a fishing line strung between their hands. Milan watched as they lifted the line over and over until a fish flapped sparkling up from the river. It was long as their brown arms, a gasping relic. One worked the hook from its mouth as the other took a plastic bag from between the rocks and they wrapped it.

Milan called to them. He wanted to know where did they sleep. They slept on the riverbank. He couldn't sleep with them but he could sleep on the riverbank: the weather was mild, some sick Americans were doing it. Milan pointed to the fish rolling in the bag. What would they do with that. Sell it to a restaurant. He asked if they thought he could get work at one of the restaurants but they made a fuss and waved him down and after that he couldn't get them to pay him any more attention.

The first night on the riverbank was very uncomfortable. Back from the cold marble slab he felt the pulse of his blood flowing as the river flowed past his padded ear without returning. From out of the dark it spun brass beneath Castel Sant' Angelo and rushed over the weir in ghostly haste. Dawn broke before he could hold his eyes shut.

¶ He worked on a building site, emptying garbage, as a waiter taking trays up and down the street and between tables. He worried about the police. He had no permit to work and he knew if they caught him they would put him on a train and fifteen hours from any given moment it would be grief, ancestry and a dry cunt all over again. Milan took precautions to blend in. He dressed down but nicely and he learned a lot of bad words and how to truncate his sentences slightly in the right places and he worked on those felt Roman vowels that are not the shrill silver of Florence or Venetian swindle or the rich buckshot of Sicily. He learned to be haughty and very polite, and he stayed out of trouble.

F

The bar where he worked was in a courtyard in Trastevere and it was busy at most hours. In the evening the lights that ran in and out of its fretted awning like a vine came on and their reflection scattered over the cobblestones as Milan approached, lurching a little with the phantom weight of concrete sacks and humming the bits of foreign music that had, years ago, returning to a radio hid under his sheets, slipped down to reside with the habit of breath. He stopped and looked up.

Tomaso was standing in the doorway of the bar watching him. Ahó, che contempli le stelle, tu?

Milan dropped his head and hurried on. He shrugged as he passed his boss in the doorway. È bella.

E tu come sei bello, eppure te pago.

Though Tomaso was apparently from an old Roman family the bar was his idea and he ran it for himself. He treated his employees well and ran a clean, safe kitchen. Milan started out washing dishes but Tomaso saw the profit in putting a suit on him and sending him out to wait tables and he was right and Milan was a success with the customers. He never asked Milan what his plans were and Milan suspected he thought he was earning money to send home.

He undressed in the bathroom and washed the last slats of dust from his armpits and from between his buttocks with his wet shirt. When he was in his uniform he rubbed a soapy thumb over his teeth then rinsed his mouth out.

From the coffee counter Tomaso pointed to a table at which a man and a woman and child had just sat down. Sarebbero der tu' paese. Nun so se pàrleno l'itajano.

Milan welcomed them and asked for their order. The man, who was extremely well dressed and whose hands moved in slim arcs as he spoke, pointed to a wine on the menu and ordered coffee and a glass of lemonade in broken Italian. The woman didn't look at either of them. She had fixed her eyes out the window and as they spoke she opened her mouth slightly without turning. The boy's chin came just above the tablecloth and his dark hair fell plumb to his eyebrows and he also stared away but it seemed to Milan to no purpose. He supposed he was their son though the man was blonde and the woman was platinum blonde.

He took them their drinks. Her lids dropped as he leaned to place the glass of lemonade before her son. She thanked him and he caught her eyes in his and nodded. Someone had crumbled a piece of bread on the tablecloth but all related hands were still as he put the drinks down. They didn't stay to finish the wine.

When Milan returned to the counter Tomaso wanted to know if he had been mistaken. Milan nodded. Sono ungheresi.

Tomaso unlocked the cash register and shook his head. He said the Eastern Europeans thought Rome was America. Pènzeno che ce farano 'n be' futuro. He pursed his lips. Hai vist'i schifosi n'i giardini, sott'i ponti. Ecco 'ndo càpiteno. Ma che futuro! Me fa sta' male 'a Roma der futuro.

   Milan said that family had money.

   Tomaso shrugged. E va be', nun è 'a stessa cosa.

¶ The woman and her son came back to the bar the following day. It was Sunday and Milan was working the afternoon. She smiled at him and said good afternoon with a good accent. Milan said hello to the boy but he didn't seem to hear. She asked Milan how long he had been working in Rome. Milan told her. Did he like it. No he didn't like to work much but he liked it here.

   She was wearing a long burgundy cardigan despite the sun falling right into the courtyard. A thin gilt chain dipped and rose over her collarbone. She ordered ice cream. When Milan brought her the bill she asked if he would be free later to take the two of them around. They had not been in town very long. It was a nice day.

   He said he would be. He met them at five o'clock on the Ponte Garibaldi. The boy was wearing an old fashioned straw hat and she had left her cardigan behind. She shielded her eyes against the sun and waved. Milan was surprised to see a pair of white canvas shoes below her dress. The two had walked out to the middle of the bridge to watch a boat passing underneath and they turned and covered half the distance as Milan approached, she leading her son by the hand, his eyes lost in his private bar of shade.

   Milan took them to the Campidoglio and if she had been already she didn't say so. She said it was very beautiful.

   They talked and walked too fast and in the museum Milan thought he might break something. The boy lagged further behind her outstretched arm as they descended the wide equestrian stairs of the Campidoglio in the bright evening.

   They walked beside the gliding river and Milan kissed her and she told him she would like to take him to a hotel and he said he agreed to everything. Her name was Magda. He followed her into the lobby of a large hotel in Prati. The concierge nodded when he saw them and took down a key from the false onyx panel behind him. The lights of the low-slung chandeliers rippled in its black sheen. Milan hesitated. She leaned and spoke into his ear, non preoccuparti. Her husband had gone home for business. He wouldn't be back for a week.

   They took the elevator and all the way she spoke to her son about the horse they had seen on the Campidoglio. It seemed he liked horses but he didn't respond. It was not a real horse. Milan thought maybe he only liked real horses.

   They left him in the sitting room by the window. In the bedroom they didn't draw the curtains. She sat at a commode by the bed and unlaced her shoes. Milan was undressed first and he leaned over her and gently pulled her dress over her head. Her breasts fell in two shallow sways across her chest. Milan stood alone and groaned and surprised them both. And there was the colour of her son's hair.

Her throat and her mouth were warm and sweat shone in the small curves. Her smell filled his mouth. He thought he pulled her down around his hips and he thought it was triumph but she took pleasure in his fast writhing and his wet blue eyes and the blind hug of his hands on her buttocks and when he came it was a gift.

¶ She watched him through her eyelashes as he picked his clothes off the floor. They had slept a little and the sun had gone down and now the lights of the city wavered through the smog the length of the window. His body gleamed in the dark from that borrowed light. The traffic hummed on the glass.

He saw her watching him and smiled. She realised that where she lay she was better illuminated than he was and the knowledge made her shut her eyes. Then he was touching some part of him to her knee and barely singing Wagon Wheel and his fingers were on her eyelids. Quanti hanni hai?

Vent'uno.

Sei sposato?

Sì.

They made love once more then he got dressed. She pulled on a robe and saw him to the door but he asked her to dinner and she said, why don't you have dinner here and stay the night. But he couldn't, he had to be at a building site early Monday, so they kissed and said goodbye. When he was gone she went over to Viktor and spoke to him and took off his straw hat and laid it on the couch.

In the morning she was up and waiting when the maid came to put a tray with their breakfast in the sitting room. She woke her son and helped him to clean and dress, then she spread jam on a piece of toast and poured him half a cup of coffee and they ate in silence. They made plans to visit a gallery but threw them up and went walking.

When they got back to the hotel there was a note at the desk from Milan. He asked her to meet him outside the lobby that evening. She paid a maid to sit with Viktor and she put her hair up with an old silver clasp that had belonged to her mother and she went down and waited by the water.

He was late. He came running in new blue jeans. He kissed her where her hair scuffed over her cheek in the wind that blew up from the river. They bought two paper cups of crushed ice and walked close together. Andiamo da te.

No, c'è la cameriera. Sta con Viktor.

He took her down some steps to the riverbank. It was cooler there and her skin thrilled. They came to a deep recess in the stone wall but she didn't want to go in. She couldn't see well but it smelled inhabited. He told her not to mind and led her with the tips of his fingers into the shadow. The sun was beginning to set over the opposite

F

bank but it was still higher than the mouth of the cave and her eyes were sunk in darkness. She felt his lips brush her ear, her cheek. He lifted her dress and her breath shot down her throat. Still he had not gone into her. She reached out and immediately her hand found his, open as if it were begging, and the lowering sun flooded the cave with light and when she jerked her head at the opening she was blinded. She blinked back in the cave.

He was hopping on bowed legs and pulling at the buttons of his new jeans and there were pots and pans hanging on the wall and rugs rolled in the corner. He grinned but he was furious. She bent deftly and slipped her knickers from her ankle and pushed them into his pocket and they left. Chi vive là?

Gli zingari.

Sarebbero arrabbiati se lo sapessero.

Sì.

Sei maleducato.

There was cement dust on his forearms. He held a hand to her hip and her dress sliding under it where an elastic had been made her long for him with infinite patience. He asked about her son. She told him about her son and her husband. He told her about the village he left and about his wife who had been old family business and much younger than him. Magda thought perhaps he was cruel to his wife. She asked him how long he planned to stay in Rome and he said forever. He said he wanted her, he wanted her to stay with him in Rome. She said that was crazy. He said he loved her and he wanted her to stay with him.

She said she had a son. They walked in silence along the riverbank until it got dark and the path filled with an electric light that cut out new shadows for them. He told her he wanted her to stay. She knew his insistence came in part from the pressure in his body and she took her hand from his and stroked the small of his back with her fingers. He could not live illegally in Rome forever.

Vero. He could take her back home. Having a wife was not such an obstacle. He could get work in the city and they would rent a flat and later buy it. He would give her a child.

They walked up onto the street and she refused to take him back to the hotel. She had left her son long enough. He told her to promise that she would see him again. She promised. Promise to let him make love to her again. She laughed in surprise and said she promised. They were tender when they said goodbye and when she looked back he was waiting.

¶ Magda's husband had returned early. She and Viktor came back to the hotel one afternoon and he was sitting in the lobby reading the newspapers. He touched Viktor on the head and kissed her.

In their room he took off his jacket and called for a bottle of whisky and one of Fanta. He talked to his son about his trip and asked after what he had seen, had he seen the Colosseum, the Forum, Neptune driving his horses over loose change. He was gentle and courteous with Viktor. Knowing what she did about his upbringing she thought he would have beaten him sometimes but he was always gentle. She sat on the couch and pushed her shoes off with her toes and tucked her legs up.

The maid came with the drinks. He filled a glass with ice and poured one for Magda. She held the glass in her lap and closed her eyes. Viktor slurped through his straw. She looked at her husband, at the fair hair swept back and the bright, elegant folds of his shirt, and felt she had almost forgotten him but looking at him could see nothing in need of remembering.

He suggested they take a stroll and choose a place to eat. At first she said she was tired, then agreed anyway. She changed into slacks and a new blouse while he shaved with the door open.

He found a bow tie in the bathroom. He stood in the doorway with half the lather scraped from his jaw and the bow tie in his hand and his braces hanging loose on his hips and looked at her. This is an old comedy thought Magda and was afraid because they had never been here before and she didn't know all the things he was capable of doing. At first they didn't speak. He was an oppressive husband but at last he said it was worth having a real holiday and went on shaving.

She knew then that he had been with other women and was surprised not to have thought of it before, and perhaps there were many other women and perhaps other children. He hadn't let his semen into her since Viktor. She felt dizzy in her guts and it was the thought she could be pregnant.

They walked, the three of them, by the river. Magda had been raised in Budapest like her husband and they had met at university. They were sweethearts for a long time before they married. He was a fine dancer and he knew Hungarian folk songs and sang them to her when they were younger. They made familiar jokes as they walked through the streets to Trastevere and Viktor laughed a beat behind with the hollow stammer of a spirit who laughs with no one.

After the others had gone to bed Magda went down to the lobby and called the number Milan had left her when they last parted. She didn't know what kind of a place the number was for. After a while a voice answered and she asked to speak to him. She heard a relay of voices then and someone else got on the phone and told her Milan wasn't there, did she want to leave a message.

The following day her husband took care of Viktor and Magda went out alone. She spent the morning in the galleries of the Villa Borghese but she was distracted and couldn't look at anything for long so she walked in the park back the way she'd come. She lingered under the trees and watched other people pass. She stopped by a fountain and leaned with one hand on the smooth pocked marble and cupped the other for the water. The sun on the broken surface dazzled her.

In the park she felt she was being followed. For some reason the concierge had warned her about the place so she left. Just outside the park she thought she saw Milan at a bus stop but when she turned back to check he was gone. There was only a man waiting with his cap pulled down over one ear and his hands in his pockets. Later, as she made her way along Via del Tritone, she thought she saw Milan reflected before her in the glass door of a wine cellar. He wasn't there when she turned. She turned again and he wasn't there. She walked all the way to the river.

Police cars were parked around the entrance to the Ponte Vittorio Emanuele II and people had gathered to look. She joined them in peering over the bridge. It seemed a gypsy had fallen in a whirlpool and drowned. Some of his people, family perhaps, stood below them on the bank talking to a police officer. They nodded and pointed tacitly. Magda heard a woman beside her say he was a good swimmer but he fell in the wrong place and they hadn't found his body. Maybe it would turn up at sea. The river swept under them in fast green curls.

Magda glanced at the faces around her and moved on. At the end of the bridge a young punk held out a rattling tin and his mutt tangled harmlessly in her legs. She dropped him fifty cents and turned towards the boulevard to San Pietro. All along the footpath tourists waited in line for the Basilica and merchants sat at easels making little paintings of the view at sunset. The bells rang out for mass. Magda was hungry and wanted to find a place to stop and eat but she moved in spurts. By now she was convinced that he was following her and she turned at every corner but it was no good, the city was full of handsome unwashed boys and they all looked back. She pushed her hands through her hair. Right out of the blue sky it began to weep, and the painters packed up and ran for cover.

THE PROSAIC
SUBLIME
OF BÉLA TARR

BY

ROSE MCLAREN

I have to recognise it's cosmical; the shit is cosmical. It's not just social,
it's not just ontological, it's really huge. And that's why we expand.
(Béla Tarr, 2007)

BÉLA TARR IS A DIRECTOR who divides the field. He makes slow, stark films
about lives in which little happens, combining old-fashioned values and innovative
methods. He records the basic elements of domestic life with incongruously sweeping,
virtuoso cinematography and picks apart the rudiments of human role-play with
elaborate subtlety, coordinating gritty detail and a sense of the universal in a way that
some see as visionary and others find tedious. Jonathan Rosenbaum, the American
film critic, has dubbed Tarr a 'despiritualised Tarkovsky'. I find him a less lapsed and
more conflicted creature: a hopeful cynic or scatological mystic, whose films are as
aggressively earthbound as they are inspiring.

    Born and raised in Hungary, Béla Tarr began his directing career in the 1970s at
the Béla Balázs Studios in Budapest, where he fell in with a group of 'documentarist'
directors dedicated to representing the lives of the working class in as pared-down
and unembellished a way as possible. His early films FAMILY NEST (1979) and THE
OUTSIDER (1981) are classic examples of the school, but through the eighties he developed away from it as he absorbed the influences of European art house cinema,
particularly Rainer Werner Fassbinder and Jean-Luc Godard, and became interested
in form, composition, metaphysics and the history of film.

    In 1984 he began collaborating with the Hungarian writer László Krasznahorkai,
with whom he went on to create many of his greatest films, DAMNATION (1988),
SÁTÁNTANGÓ (1994) and WERCKMEISTER HARMONIES (2000) – these last two adapta-
tions of Krasznahorkai's novels SÁTÁNTANGÓ and THE MELANCHOLY OF RESISTANCE,
respectively. The elaborate sentences and unorthodox structures of Krasznahorkai's
novels seem to have informed Tarr's own formal innovations – the lengthy takes,
chapter divisions and sprawling psychological odysseys of which his later films are
composed. It is also in Krasznahorkai's literature that Tarr seems to have identified a
vast and surreal perspective through which to envision the lives of ordinary people.
Though the range of Tarr's artistic relationships and interests has shaped a highly
distinctive approach, it also has much to do with his cultural position. Working between Soviet-scarred Hungary and the comparatively prosperous and liberated West
seems to have afforded him a peculiarly mixed sensibility: aesthetically both Spartan
and grand and politically as aspirational as it is hopeless.

E

Tarr has only made nine feature films and claims that his most recent, *THE TURIN HORSE* (2011), will be his last. Though dogged by a cult following from his early output, it is only in the past decade that he has acquired a fuller fan-base, starting with Artificial Eye's release of his films on DVD and culminating in the Jury Grand Prix award for *THE TURIN HORSE*, co-written with Krasznahorkai, at the Berlin Film Festival in 2011. Yet he is still little known and much misunderstood. If his latest film is indeed to be his last, he surely deserves an appraisal that debunks the myths surrounding his work and celebrates what he has discreetly created. The shit *is* cosmical: he has made for cinema a prosaic sublime.

His is an art form of dissolving contrasts in which the everyday lives of individuals are located within the broader frameworks of politics and nature. Minutiae are shown to contain the seeds of power, survival or despair, and the vile or banal is filmed with astonishing sensitivity. This is an essentially disproportionate worldview that pits paradox against conventional logic, taste or taxonomy. It follows the effects of huge historical, even meteorological forces on tiny populations; it proves that beauty can inhere in something as simple as wood grain; and it suggests different ways in which to conceive of, even perhaps accept, cruelty and boredom. Alternatively it witnesses how such sliding scales and acute contrasts might provoke madness or revelation. In *THE TURIN HORSE* there is a long, luminous chiaroscuro close-up of a steaming baked potato. In isolation it might seem bland, indulgent or absurd, but in the story's context of desperate hunger, the messianic splendour of the vegetable makes sense. In this way the excesses or eccentricities of Tarr's vision have a function in depicting lives distorted by hardship or isolation. This gloss of the prosaic sublime sheds light on the director by elucidating the ways in which apparently contradictory, inappropriate, fanciful or gratuitously depressing elements in his work also have radical meaning.

¶ Typically, Béla Tarr's films follow the decline of small, poor, rural communities in Eastern Europe, as in *DAMNATION*, *WERCKMEISTER HARMONIES* and *SÁTÁNTANGÓ*. These are often construed as dystopian fables on the fall of communism and understood in terms of Tarr's Hungarian nationality. His films are artefacts of his country's post-communist existence and the need to communicate this is a major motive for his film-making. He has said of *WERCKMEISTER HARMONIES*, 'I have a hope, if you watch this film, you understand something about our life, about what is happening in middle Europe, how we are living there, in a kind of edge of the world.' Yet his scripts and direction suggest at an immediate level a less politically pointed and more general agenda. There are no named locations or historical references in his work. When he talks about 'the shit' he has clarified that he means the human condition, not the Hungarian situation. Shot in villages and taking the form of a folk tale or twisted morality play in the manner of Lars von Trier's *DOGVILLE*, his films are the stories

E

of any sublunar striving. Prosaic in subject, style and appeal, they are about common experience.

Most of Béla Tarr's characters are mired in shit of some kind or other. His films are usually set in unforgiving landscapes and grim weather. There is barely a dry shot in *DAMNATION*, with its backdrop of epic rain and its foreground of mud. *THE TURIN HORSE* unfolds on a bare steppe whipped by spectacularly strong winds. And his magnum opus *SÁTÁNTANGÓ* is a whorling world of grey skies and sodden earth through which the locals hopelessly grope.

These surroundings are atmospheric but to mention pathetic fallacy here would imply a distinction entirely absent from Tarr's artistic vision. In the literary device, a character's surroundings reflect their thoughts or feelings; in Tarr's films there is no such divide and no such mirroring. For him, the material make-up of life constitutes a soul as much as anything else and to understand Tarr's outlook is not to analyse but to enter into the physical experiences of his actors. This isn't difficult, for his films are powerfully visceral, the weather and sets as deeply textured and evocative as any words or personalities. I emerged from *THE TURIN HORSE* feeling as storm-battered as moved. The effects are necessarily related: the harsh conditions in which the two protagonists live underwrite the brute simplicity of their relationship.

In all of Tarr's films there is a strong synthesis between the basic elements of a place and the psychology of its people. The landscape and characters are wholly unified, transcending metaphorical distinctions. In *SÁTÁNTANGÓ* the muck underfoot and the filthy politics of village life are of a piece; enduring the bodily toils of a rustic existence and resisting the parochial backslide into vice are part of the same struggle. It is in this context that his characters acquire a certain stature: not so much a matter of surviving in spite of circumstances as of living through them.

Regarding the sublime, his work certainly contains enough horror to court the darker sense of the word: the provocation of awe and fear that Enlightenment philosophers inscribed in the term. But Tarr inverts the inherited understanding, locating irrational terror in the deeply primitive rather than in the spiritual. *SÁTÁNTANGÓ*, as its title might suggest, is a carnivalesque of the lower depths. A brother robs his little sister of her pittance pocket money. She in turn tortures a cat to death, then poisons herself – and meanwhile the villagers scheme, drink, dance and fuck themselves senseless over twelve chapters that gyre and descend like so many spirals of hell. *WERCKMEISTER HARMONIES* reaches a more acute climax, in which the locals vandalise a hospital and abuse its patients, in one of the least explicit but most disturbing scenes in the history of cinematic violence.

Yet for all their raw brutality, Béla Tarr's films are also surprisingly full of wonder: from the mystery of the ringing bells in *SÁTÁNTANGÓ* to the glorious enigma of the whale in *WERCKMEISTER HARMONIES*. Otherwise relentlessly harsh narratives are interrupted by marvels, all the more marvellous for their unlikely settings. Though these incidents tend to come from nature or folk mythology, they bring into play forces beyond human comprehension, adding an extraordinary and uplifting dimension to Tarr's world.

There is also a much nearer form of the sublime in his work in the ideal of dignity, which stands as a godless equivalent to salvation and an alternative to the easier secular lodestars of romance, success or celebrity. These forms of redemption all tend to arrive via some *deus ex machina*, but Tarr would prefer his characters to acquire their own grace. As he told Howard Feinstein, 'All our movies is [*sic*] talking about the human dignity and I think this is the point of view which is the main issue.' He complains that the word has fallen into disuse and it is as if his films attempt to rescue the concept from dour worthiness or sanctimony and rearticulate not only the importance but the beauty – glamour, even – of dignity. The singer in *DAMNATION* is a heroine in this vein, a woman eking out a melancholy existence in a backwater town with a miraculous degree of style. She has liquidly greasy hair; she moans and groans at the local dive for a living; we even watch her give her boss a blowjob under the bar. And yet, against all odds, she maintains a livelihood, as well as her sex appeal, charisma and integrity. As she tells her would-be lover, Kamer, 'I know that I'm alone, I know it well, but I'll not give up,' – which pillow talk amounts to the moral of this particular story, or the closest we ever get to one. More flexible and modulated than stoicism: an individual's means of coping within society with their own rough forms of physical and ethical elegance.

In *ARTFORUM*, James Quandt wrote that Béla Tarr's films are often about escapes, made or missed. This offers a potential key to his world, but only as a kind of inverse truth. Tarr handles any kind of 'beyond' with a blunt scepticism; where escape is mooted, it is more a myth or a parody of reality than a possibility. In *DAMNATION* and *SÁTÁNTANGÓ*, characters long and attempt to flee their miserable homes, but are prevented, more often by a lack of alternatives than by a lack of courage. Flight becomes increasingly irrelevant as a solution to the states of social or psychological despair that characters suffer. Sorrow is ubiquitous; shifting ground a red herring and, moreover, a cop-out, both as a plot-device and life-decision. Escape is never an option, but it does throw those available into relief. Surviving with as much humanity as you can muster is often the best, or only, course. Happily, this doubles as a practical solution for his characters and a value system for Tarr, synthesising both his neorealist and his ideological ambitions by conferring a naturalistic heroism on characters who do what they have to.

So far so serious, but Tarr is also the master of a dry, dark type of comedy and underlying any hope in his films is a cynicism that fuels their black humour. There are no dead baby gags but the gung-ho bawdiness with which the cast of *SÁTÁNTANGÓ*

E

inevitably decline does curl the corners of the mouth – if curving closer to a grimace. There is also a kind of slow, sadomasochistic joke in the absurd length of the tragedies Tarr drags himself and his viewers through. Both *DAMNATION* and *SÁTÁNTANGÓ* feature strung-out bar scenes in which the revellers all eventually depart or pass out, leaving a last man standing in the early hours to the mock-glorious strains of an accordion. The music mimics a wink at the audience, sending up and garlanding the drunkard's perseverance, while simultaneously burlesquing the viewer's stamina. Like the punters, you can always leave, but you probably won't.

¶ Tarr is famous, or infamous, for staggeringly long takes. *SÁTÁNTANGÓ* runs at over 7 hours and is made of only 150 takes. He would have them longer if he could, complaining that his only limit is the length of Kodak film, which stretches to 300m, about 11 minutes. This is extremely unusual by today's standards – the average take now lasts but a few seconds – making his films challenging to watch and urging some justification for their length. To an extent, the dilatory nature of his films is a way of celebrating (and demanding) endurance. More importantly though, it effects a kind of durational empathy. Watching *DAMNATION* or *SÁTÁNTANGÓ* creates a strong impression of what life must be like in such hamlets – like watching paint not dry.

There is a crucial difference, though, between an art form that conveys ennui and suffering and an art form that is just painfully boring. Tarr's prodigious talent as a visual director is perhaps the necessary complement to the time he takes as the awesome beauty of the cinematography in his films renders them (almost) endlessly watchable. And while I don't agree with Susan Sontag that *SÁTÁNTANGÓ* is 'enthralling for every minute of its seven hours', I do think it is exquisite to *look* at for its entire duration. There are the spectral portraits of Esti, slow pale shots, almost quivering stills, that communicate the bleached-out blankness of her existence more powerfully than any words might; or those sequences where the camera stalks characters walking to and from the village, through landscapes so magnificently bleak you perversely yearn to be there; and then, of course, the orgiastic pub scene at the heart of the film, a figurative grotesque as repulsively seductive as anything Hieronymus Bosch or David Lynch might dream up.

Tarr is certainly not the puritan some of his directorial dogma might suggest. Far from the asceticism of his early documentarist approach, his later cinematography is always aesthetically appealing and his narratives full of comedy, cynicism, brawling, lust and artistic reference. In his mature work he appropriates painters (Bruegel, Caravaggio, Vermeer, van Gogh) and cinematic tropes like the overt noirishness of *DAMNATION* and *THE MAN FROM LONDON*. Music also becomes increasingly important; *WERCKMEISTER HARMONIES'* title refers to a baroque music theorist and the need to recalibrate harmony. Mihály Víg's musical scores play no small part in the

E

film, providing simple but soaring accompaniments that stay in keeping with the tone, as do his expansive compositions for *SATÁNTANGÓ* and *THE TURIN HORSE*.

This is all quite awkward. On one hand, Tarr appears to insist on rugged honesty and on the other he makes films that are operatic in their artistic complexity and ambition. He snubs the loftiness of Art with a capital A but claims all mainstream cinema is 'shit' (and presumably not cosmical). Yet, though Tarr does evade categorisation, this would appear to be less an obtuse pose for the critics and more a straightforward reflection of his attitude and peculiarity as a director. His films are unique. They don't cleave to the redemptive structures of Hollywood romance and have little of the speed, wit, décor or lifestyle references that distance many indie films from reality and imbue them with a richness absent from it. Bresson, Godard or Rainer Werner Fassbinder may not rose-tint their worlds, but they do culturally console both their characters and their viewers. You might feel sad or outcast in any of their films, but at least you have the comfort of being unquestionably cool with it. They offer the lonely some sense of belonging to a set of aesthetics.

Tarr's films seem to work the other way; they are about the qualities of individuals within groups rather than what he would see as the false yoke of plot or vogue. A cited influence here is Bruegel. In a *KINOEYE* interview Tarr discusses his admiration for the painter's talent for drawing out the peculiar nature of each figure in a crowd, saying, 'Everyone has a personality. That's the reason I like Bruegel and that's what I learned from him.'

There is a scene at the end of *WERCKMEISTER HARMONIES* which feels like an homage to the old master: a local community is filmed standing outside the village hall. The framing and composition recall scenes typical of the painter. An overall effect of unity is conveyed in long-distance shots of panoramic width that survey the ragged group in its entirety, before a long close-up sequence that examines the individuals and their relations to one another in detail, the camera moving slowly from one face to the next, every one an index of responses to the collective drama they have each taken part in and witnessed. The scene is strangely affecting, yet all it does is affirm the place of these rather compromised individuals within their world. Nothing has been distorted, explained, resolved or promised, but something has been quietly fêted.

Bruegel magnified the rudimentary and in this respect is an obvious precursor to Tarr. And yet, the director would rail against any such status, claiming, 'For me, the biggest danger is somebody telling me you are an artist.' Though the prosaic elements in his work make some sense of his paranoia, I suspect a degree of stubbornness, even mendacity, in his anti-art posturing. It is impossible to watch his films without observing how strikingly beautiful they are and this is no coincidence – most of them take years to make and the production is painstaking. It isn't unmotivated – beauty

E

clearly has a function for him. Tarr might not want to spin illusions or sanctify any squalor, and he certainly isn't courting the cinematic canon, but he does want to dignify his subjects and appears to do so through a profoundly poetic visual language. Denying himself or his work an artistic status seems extremely unconvincing and unnecessary. Why might he maintain such a position?

At a strategic level, it looks defensive. His work eludes the zeitgeist, being too down to earth for fashion; too simple for intellectualism; and too earnest for irony. Wooing the contemporary art scene would probably prove a vain pursuit. More fundamentally, though, he appears chary of the critical discourse that is now the lifeblood of contemporary culture (if also vampiric), and there is an extent to which he might downplay the credentials and media coverage of his films to preserve their autonomy, the primacy of what he calls a 'primitive language'. The prevailing truth of the matter, though, is that he doesn't give a shit what anyone thinks. Which isn't indifference; it's a gesture of faith in his work.

The real shame of this silence is that it generates misconceptions. Worst among them, Susan Sontag's recruitment of his films as 'heroic violations of the norm' in her moribund–lament–cum–lofty–rant about the decay of film standards and the dying super–species of cinéastes. Though Tarr is anti–establishment, Sontag's is precisely the sort of counter–conversation he doesn't want to enter, her 'Death of Cinephilia' another wave of crusading hysteria turning him agnostic. Cinema is not dead, and he would rather prove it by making films than talking about them or joining a cause. And if *THE TURIN HORSE* is to be his final film, I suspect it is also the last we will hear from him, marking an apparent immunity to the reception of his work that is, again, quite unusual.

Working outside of any local, mainstream, art house or realist collective makes him something of an anomaly. By choosing not to take part in today's creative dialogues and eschewing the cultural milieu within which his films have to exist (they need to be screened to be seen), he runs the risk of making films that are less immediately relevant to their audiences, but in the hope that they ultimately have a broader reach. A new set of ideals emerges through this cinema, a prosaic sublime. Unmodish and of epic scope, it is Everyman's art.

E

INTERVIEW

WITH

CHINA MIÉVILLE

IT IS A CLICHÉ TO SAY THAT A WRITER'S WORK resists classification. It is ironic then that China Miéville, among the most ambitious, imaginative and unconventional novelists at work in the world today, should so actively endorse his own writing's categorisation by genre. A three-time winner of the prestigious Arthur C. Clarke Award for science fiction, Miéville has since the publication of his debut novel *KING RAT* in 1998 achieved a level of critical and commercial success that the literary establishment is apt to characterise as an ascent from the ghetto of genre fiction. Yet he remains avowedly a writer of science fiction and fantasy, and one among an increasingly influential group of authors operating outside the parameters of 'literary fiction', that most tautological and self-denying of styles. The energy, experimentalism and intellectual radicalism of novels such as *IRON COUNCIL* – described by the *WASHINGTON POST* as an 'elegiac paean to Utopian socialism, romantic revolutionaries and the European radical tradition' – reminds us of the artificiality of any distinction between historic 'genre' writers such as Philip K. Dick, M. John Harrison or H. P. Lovecraft and those equally nonconformist fabulists such as Jonathan Swift, Jorge Luis Borges and J. G. Ballard who have been afforded the recognition of the canon.

The author of ten novels, including three works in the Bas-Lag series that takes its name from the fictional world in which it is set, Miéville's recent masterpiece *EMBASSYTOWN* typifies his ability to marry the construction of a fantastic universe to the exploration of an idea. This is a story about the dangerously intoxicating capacities of language, expressed in the prose of a writer himself in thrall to the possibilities offered by vocabulary, metaphor and simile. Ursula K. Le Guin wrote of the book that it 'works on every level, providing compulsive narrative, splendid intellectual rigour and risk, moral sophistication, fine verbal fireworks and sideshows, and even the old-fashioned satisfaction of watching a protagonist become more of a person than she gave promise of being'. The same qualities are evident in *THE CITY AND THE CITY*, which presents the reader with an urban landscape inhabited by two independent populations, each forced to 'unsee' the other or risk punishment by Breach. Its noir prose is allied to the narrative structure of a police procedural, while the atmosphere is of an Eastern European capital under occupation. Yet the work transcends these referents and frameworks to achieve a moral and intellectual complexity that renders most 'realist' fiction (another unhelpful term) lazy and insular by comparison.

A left-wing activist, Miéville ran unsuccessfully for parliament on behalf of the Socialist Alliance in London in 2001 and five years later published the self-explanatorily titled *BETWEEN EQUAL RIGHTS: A MARXIST THEORY OF INTERNATIONAL LAW*. In 2012 he published *LONDON'S OVERTHROW*, an expanded, illustrated version of 'Oh, London, You Drama Queen', an editorial written in advance of the London Olympics for the *NEW YORK TIMES*. In person he is both patient and excitable, exhibiting the same generosity of spirit and wide flung intellectual curiosity that makes his writing so exhilarating.

Q· THE WHITE REVIEW — When did you begin to consider the possibility of a career as a writer? I ask because you studied Social Anthropology and later International Relations, and seemed set to pursue a career as an academic. Did you write fiction from a young age?

A· CHINA MIÉVILLE — I actually began by studying English at university, but I switched to Social Anthropology after about a term. In a sense, all I wanted to do was to write fiction, but I was aware that it was a big ask to make a career out of it. I enjoyed academia, but felt a slightly wistful sense of aspiration about the writing until it began to take off, in the second year of my Ph.D. I still enjoy trying to be, semi–peripherally, a part of that academic world.

Q· THE WHITE REVIEW — What was it about the study of English at university that so immediately put you off the subject?

A· CHINA MIÉVILLE — Simply that the structure of the course at Cambridge didn't float my boat. In particular, what I would later understand to be critical theory was largely absent from the curriculum. I knew about theory in a very hazy sense and was interested by it. Anthropology at that time was overtly, inextricably bound up in critical theory, which made it more attractive to me. Had I been at an institution in which the study of English had been more overtly theoretical and politicised, then I might have stayed with it. There's no sectarianism against the subject – I'm not one of these people who thinks that the study of literature ruins anything, that's a silly position – but it didn't work for me in that time and place. In retrospect I'm glad, because the study of Social Anthropology and then International Relations has been enormously important to me, politically and theoretically.

Q· THE WHITE REVIEW — It's often said that studying English encourages a more insular style of writing: literature that is about literature. Is an academic background outside of that conducive to creating fiction that is more outward looking, more engaged with the world?

A· CHINA MIÉVILLE — Well, you should do both. If you're interested in genre, as I am, then you're always in discussion with generic traditions. Talking to earlier fiction is talking to, and arguing with, the earlier world.

Q· THE WHITE REVIEW — In your work there is an overarching affiliation to the science fiction and fantasy genre, but within that you play with other genre types. In *IRON COUNCIL*, for instance, you appropriate – if that's the right word – the model of the Western. I'm interested in that tension between adopting the frameworks, their tropes, and then somewhat adapting them to suit your own purposes.

A· CHINA MIÉVILLE — Well the first thing to say is that I have nothing but love and respect for the science fiction and fantasy tradition because it's what formed me in literary terms. One doesn't want to be constrained by it, not in the sense that genre need necessarily be a straitjacket, but just in the sense that one doesn't want to be restricted to a single position. Neither would I want to be constrained by the genre that you might call literary fiction. Every writer will have his or her favourites, and I will always gravitate towards the fantastic, but that doesn't preclude a writer from being interested in other things.

Q· THE WHITE REVIEW — But does that willingness to look beyond the constraints of a genre not irk hardcore science fiction and fantasy fans?

A· CHINA MIÉVILLE — The geek community does tend towards a sense of embattlement.

There is certainly resentment towards writers who seem to write in a genre and then distance themselves from it, as if they're kicking the muck off their coat. I have a relatively easy ride in that respect because I don't kick the muck off, I relish it, I love the tradition that formed me and of which I am a part.

Saying that, I'm tired of this embattlement. For a long time there has, perfectly legitimately, been a lot of anger about the snobbery of the mainstream towards certain generic traditions and protocols. I share that, but I also think that we should shut up and get on. Things are now more open than they have been for a very long time. When kids complain about genres being ignored... I mean seriously, are you watching TV or reading newspapers? This is bullshit, we have never been so prominent as a tradition.

I don't want us to stay underground, I'm not interested in gutter chic, but I do worry that there is the danger that we as a community will become complacent. Having complained for so long about being ignored by the mainstream, I now feel it's time to take some lessons. There's a younger generation of writers within the tradition that are a lot more open-minded, so I'm optimistic about the future. There is a lot of interesting cross-fertilisation going on.

^{Q.} THE WHITE REVIEW —— You've become something of a figurehead and spokesman for your genre, at least partly because your readership extends far beyond its traditional audience. Are you conscious of writing for people that might not normally read science fiction or fantasy?
^{A.} CHINA MIÉVILLE —— I have become aware that people often say to me, 'I don't normally read this kind of thing, but I read your book and really liked it,' which is very nice. I welcome that not because I want to escape a traditional science fiction readership, but because it does matter to me to be read: I want to be read by as many people as possible. That isn't to say that I would write something with a view to maximising reader numbers at the expense of a certain tradition, simply because that wouldn't interest me as a writer. I don't have any desire to leave the tradition of the fantastic behind. I would much rather use my position to point out that there are plenty of other writers from within this tradition who people might also like.

^{Q.} THE WHITE REVIEW —— Does it bore you to have to answer questions about genre? The very notion of a critically-acclaimed fantasy writer is sometimes treated as exotic by the literary establishment – is that frustrating? I lapse into it because it *is* exciting and also slightly mortifying, for a reader like me, to read your works because they have to some degree penetrated the critical mainstream, and then to investigate further, and realise there is this whole field of great writing about which I know relatively little.

^{A.} CHINA MIÉVILLE —— No, having someone say what you just said is really moving, it means a huge amount. There are some questions that you resent having to answer, but generally what I do fear is becoming boring. One has to retire particular riffs. When I was younger I said various things about Tolkien, explaining in a swaggering, young, punky way why I disliked his work. Then, when I would go to conventions people began to say, 'China, do the Tolkien thing!' So you have to stop. It's the same with some of the recurring themes in my fiction. I'm fanatically interested in rubbish, and I'm fanatically interested in cephalopods and houses and things like that, so I have to police myself. 'No more cephalopods for three books, no more garbage until 2016,' that sort of

thing, because otherwise you risk self-parody.

^{Q.} THE WHITE REVIEW —— The influence of London on your work is another recurring theme. It's always loomed large, from your debut novel KING RAT, through many of the short stories collected in LOOKING FOR JAKE, and most explicitly in LONDON'S OVERTHROW. There seems to be a lot of London in the city-state of New Crobuzon, too, the setting for PERDIDO STREET STATION, the first of your Bas-Lag novels. Do you consider yourself to be a writer of London, in the same way that, say, Iain Sinclair could be considered a writer of London?

^{A.} CHINA MIÉVILLE —— I think so. London looms extremely large in society, it feels formative in the way that I neither can nor wish to escape from, and writers like Sinclair are hugely important to me. London's one of those cities that filters a particularly intense and hallucinatory aesthetic and I feel very formed by that, I suspect I am very much a London writer. Writing LONDON'S OVERTHROW was quite moving, quite affecting, because it was the first time I had explicitly addressed London in non-fiction.

I'm particularly interested in the city's inclusions and its exclusions, in who gets left out of London. One thing about the tradition you've touched upon is that it is very gendered. The names that always crop up are Iain Sinclair, Peter Ackroyd, Thomas de Quincey, Alan Moore… They are interesting and important writers, but where are Emma Tennant, Jane Gaskell, Mary Butts?

^{Q.} THE WHITE REVIEW —— Laura Oldfield Ford?

^{A.} CHINA MIÉVILLE —— Yes, I feel like her star is waxing, which is terrific, and I wonder if she's going to start being mentioned in the same breath as those writers. It feels to me like a tradition that has been gendered for a long time, so I hope that the next phase of that lineage of London visionaries is to reclaim voices that should never have been left out.

^{Q.} THE WHITE REVIEW —— One of the things that I found fascinating about LONDON'S OVERTHROW was that I could trace the preoccupations with urban society that you explore in your fiction. Themes of hybridity, and the intermixture of classes and cultures as a positive aspect of urban living. You talked about the way that London encourages inclusion and exclusion, and some of your fiction presents cities in which two tribes or cultures co-exist but are unable, or barred from, interacting with each other. Your short graphic story ON THE WAY TO THE FRONT, illustrated by Liam Sharp, has soldiers from a foreign war passing through London but remaining almost invisible to its inhabitants. In THE CITY AND THE CITY two populations occupy the same geographical space but are discouraged from perceiving, and banned from acknowledging, each other. It's easy to draw parallels with the organisation of society in London. Are you consciously making a statement about the way we interact? Are you setting out from that point?

^{A.} CHINA MIÉVILLE —— Inevitably, parallels can be drawn but I don't think that's what the fiction is for, in any narrow sense. I'm not interested in allegorical fiction, except to the extent that allegorical fiction can escape itself. I'm fascinated by ecstatic religious writers, poets like Francis Thompson or George MacDonald. He writes these phantasies, clearly religious allegories, and they get stranger and stranger, and where the allegory breaks down is where they become interesting. It becomes metaphor, which is inherently proliferative and unstable.

A piece of fiction like THE CITY AND THE

CITY inevitably has metaphorical resonance for the way we live in our own city, because that's what it came out of. But I certainly didn't think, 'Oooh, now to write a novel that will coolly point out how we ignore each other all the time.' A statement like that is a banality. So that formulation you use – 'making a statement' – is one that makes me flinch, as is 'sending a message', as is 'making a point'.

It's difficult, because critics that I respect have on occasion accused me of letting my fiction run away from the world because it doesn't set out to make these points in a systematic way, and to me that's simply not what fiction does. I'm not saying that it never can, I do think there is such a thing as good agitprop fiction, though I think it's rare. But I don't think that this is the only means by which fiction can be politically interesting. That's just nuts! You read something like, and I'm not comparing myself here, but you read something like Kafka's 'The Cares of a Family Man', the story of Odradek. Clearly that's a story which in its very essence evades simple decoding, but the idea that it's therefore politically uninteresting and banal is just gobsmacking to me. That's an extreme example because the story is almost defined by its opacity, but I think that what we should be looking for is resonances. With respect to what you were saying about my own fiction, it's true that those resonances are there, and while I welcome them and think they're formative to the fiction I don't want to appear to be making a point. I simply don't think that is what fiction is for. If I want to make a point I'll just make a point. Fiction is much more interesting for being saturated with that stuff while being irreducible to it.

Q. THE WHITE REVIEW — *EMBASSYTOWN* seems to in some way dramatise the collapse of allegory into metaphor.

A. CHINA MIÉVILLE — Yes, very much so. I had been thinking for some years about writing a book about metaphor, a scholarly book. I would still like to, in fact. I have a shelf of books on the subject, and on my e-book reader a little file full of texts about metaphor. It's partly a question of time, partly a question of focus, and partly the fact that I think I'm first and foremost a fiction writer. That's the way my mind works, so I slowly realised that this other story I'd been thinking about for many years, about double-voiced aliens, lent itself very well to a dramatisation of some of those same ideas about metaphor. There is the added advantage with fiction, and this goes back to what we were just talking about, that you don't have to come to a conclusion. You raise questions without deciding the answers, and you can pin narrative hooks on ideas which taken literally you know to be wrong. The ideas themselves, their scientific accuracy, don't matter. The fact that a theory is wrong doesn't mean you can't do very interesting things with it in fictional terms. There was a certain kind of relief in realising that I could investigate these things in fictional form, through this story that I'd been trying to write for literally decades.

Q. THE WHITE REVIEW — There's an interesting tension in *EMBASSYTOWN*, and in other of your works, between the breakdown and disruption of language – which might traditionally be considered a preoccupation of the literary avant-garde – and a tightly plotted narrative framework.

A. CHINA MIÉVILLE — Well, that's a really productive tension. I come out of a plot tradition in which narrative is very important, but at the same time I'm interested in the avant-garde tradition of anti-narrative and fractured narrative. My fiction does tend, to varying degrees, to be very plot-driven, but I also get frustrated by the idea that narrative is hardwired into us as human beings. Even if narrative is hard-wired into us, that doesn't mean it's good. It's too obvious to point out how invidious is the narrativisation of politics.

A healthy suspicion about narrative does not preclude us from enjoying it. We simply should not proceed from the assumption that our predilection for making stories out of chaos is a good thing.

Q. THE WHITE REVIEW — In *EMBASSYTOWN* language becomes an addictive toxin, responsible for the breakdown of society. Language is a concrete thing, a dangerous substance, and that premise is very similar to that of Ben Marcus' *THE FLAME ALPHABET*, in which language is poisonous. Is there a trend towards questioning the value of language?

A. CHINA MIÉVILLE — I wanted to question language as a set of references. I mean, the idea of language as potentially not such a good thing isn't new. You've got films like *PONTYPOOL*, even Laurie Anderson's 'Language is a Virus'. It's not a new idea, but I do think it's an interesting one.

I would like to make a slight conceptual difference between language and narrative, and the question of whether language is a positive or a negative thing. I think that question is unanswerable. There are some radical positions: you could say it all went wrong with symbolic thought. I wouldn't take that position, but I wouldn't reduce language to narrative. Part of the thing that narrative does which is problematic is exactly that reduction. I think it's Deleuze who talks about 'language as a means of coercion', which I may have quoted in *EMBASSYTOWN* without attribution [the line in *EMBASSYTOWN* is 'language is the continuation of coercion by other means'].

There's this mainstream idea that language is born out of a necessity for communication, and then there's this rather pleasingly provocative idea that language is born out of the exigencies of coercion. It's the job of philosophers to decide which of those theories are true, but both of them can be productive for fiction. *EMBASSYTOWN* was partly an attempt to mediate that in fiction.

Q. THE WHITE REVIEW — If we accept this idea that language reifies power frameworks and power structures inherent in society, then is there a responsibility for the fiction writer to play with language? To challenge the structures of language?

A. CHINA MIÉVILLE — I am reluctant to say that the fiction writer has any responsibilities beyond those that we all have as decent human beings. If you're a writer or a reader who enjoys straight fiction with traditional language, I think there's nothing wrong with that.

I personally am interested in fiction and indeed poetry that doesn't take language for granted. This is one of the ways in which we can return to the genre tradition. There's a mainstream position according to which language is a clear glass window, and there's a story behind it, and you see through the language to the story. There's always been a smaller but very important counter-tradition of what we call modernism, or postmodernism. It's most overt in the experimentalism of people like Samuel R. Delany, but equally there are writers like Kathy Acker who in the most flamboyant way turns language on its head, for whom it is absolutely not a clear window. As a writer and a reader I like that tradition that doesn't take language for granted, but I wouldn't call it a responsibility, I would call it a predilection.

Q· THE WHITE REVIEW —— I'm quite intrigued by your reluctance to impose responsibilities on the writer.

A· CHINA MIÉVILLE —— Why?

Q· THE WHITE REVIEW —— Because typically we all like to think that there are certain kinds of duties inherent in what we do, there's a certain vanity in believing that there's a right way and a wrong way, and that you're doing it the right way.

A· CHINA MIÉVILLE —— Well this is not political or stylistic relativism, or a laissez-faire thing. I'm highly critical of lots of works, and although I wouldn't put it in deontological terms as you did, I certainly think that there are things that I want writers to do and there are things that I don't want writers to do.

Q· THE WHITE REVIEW —— What don't you want them to do?

A· CHINA MIÉVILLE —— I don't want them to unquestioningly replicate tropes and ideologies, which happens all the fucking time. To be clear, it's not just writers who do this, and I don't like segmenting off writers as if they were a cadre of specialists, but I don't like fiction which unthinkingly others certain groups of people. Anything that treats Muslims as ethnicised scapegoats, or pathologises homosexuality, or women's desire, or replicates Horatio Alger bullshit about class, that troubles me because I don't like it in the real world

It is possible to be blown away by a piece of art as an hallucinatory expression of a position with which you disagree - HEART OF DARKNESS, for example, is among many outstanding works of art saturated with reactionary positions. I am more frustrated with art that is unthinking. I imagine that's why a lot of people on the Left are more interested in modernism, which is very reactionary. Modernism may be motivated by reactionary ideas, but it doesn't take them for granted. Liberal fiction, on the other hand, is often guilty of repeating nostrums and embedding liberal assumptions.

Q· THE WHITE REVIEW —— Is that point not related to what you were saying about language – the unthinking adoption of words and phrases? In LONDON'S OVERTHROW you discuss the word feral, and its application by certain parts of the British press to the nation's youth. The phrase 'feral youth' is so embedded in our culture now that its usage has become unthinking. I think the attraction of modernism to contemporary writers is that, although it might be an expression of a reactionary political position, it's also a challenge to received ideas.

A· CHINA MIÉVILLE —— The introduction of the word feral was not accidental, there was a deliberate agenda behind that, and the fact that it is unthinkingly reproduced now is awful. But while there are some words that are now given, there are others that have become ungiven, epithets you can no longer use, which I think represents progress. The fact that 'coloured' is no longer an acceptable term strikes me as a social triumph.

I certainly wouldn't want to go down the route of saying that modernism was only utilised by reactionaries, that's clearly untrue. I think in fact that things are changing quite abruptly – even over the past two years I've seen a greater open-mindedness. It's a cause for national literary shame that writers like Ann Quin have been neglected for so long. It's symptomatic of a longstanding antipathy to modernism within the mainstream literary culture of this country which is now slowly being overturned.

The scandal around the Booker Prize in 2011 [when the judges nominated 'readability' as a criteria for assessing the best book] was interesting because it exposed the connection between this country's traditional scepticism towards the avant–garde and an ostentatiously middlebrow sensibility. The link between those two things had always been implicit, but had previously been disavowed. I don't want to suggest that you *have* to be middlebrow to be anti-modernist, but I think that has been the tradition here.

There's no doubt that the kind of statements made by the Booker judges in 2011, and which are typical within the field of mainstream literary fiction, are unthinkable in the case of, for example, the Prix Goncourt. The idea of a Goncourt judge saying that they are looking for fiction that zips along is laughable.

Q THE WHITE REVIEW —— You've said previously: 'I've tried to instrumentalise a certain lack of aesthetic discipline in my own approach to writing.' Your style shifts from book to book, in its tone and the adoption of different perspectives, but there is this consistently maximalist approach to the sentence. That is something which seems very exciting after forty-odd years in which the predominant, though not universal, mode has been towards paring down sentences. In the same interview you say, 'The whole kind of "kill your darlings" cliché of writing is a very good injunction – but at the same time, sometimes I think, well, actually, let that darling live.'

A CHINA MIÉVILLE —— As a writer and a reader I'm at least as interested in maximalism as minimalism. I've always been frustrated by the givens of creative writing courses, 'kill your darlings', 'eradicate adjectives', 'eradicate adverbs'. Of course there are great books written on that basis, but the idea that this is what one should do with writing strikes me as absolutely bizarre. I really like Lars Iyer, his blog and his essays and his books, and his essay after literature especially ['Nude in Your

Hot Tub', published on THE WHITE REVIEW website in 2011]. But at the end of that essay, when he's wondering if it's hopeless to write now, he instead offers us guidelines, one of which is 'kill your adverbs'. No! None of this follows. Kill your adverbs if you want to, and if you don't, don't.

I have at times, and particularly in THE CITY AND THE CITY, employed a more restrained style. You know, even the adjectives which we have to describe that style are ideological. The most popular adjective is 'spare' – spare writing. As if there's a certain number of words in the world, and that if someone uses too many of them there's going to be a word shortage. It's absurd. Another word is 'precise'. I mean, precise in what? If you say the word table, the word table is no more table-like than the phrase 'old eldritch brown table'. Neither are them are remotely table-like. The idea of the *mot juste* is in some sense a terrible idea. One of the main things about language is that there is no *mot juste*; language is not the world.

Q THE WHITE REVIEW —— I want to finish with a simple question, that we always put to authors for the benefit of any aspiring writers who might be reading. It's about the process of writing, the practicalities of pursuing writing as a career. I don't want to ask you what your favourite pencil is, but can you give us an insight into how you put each book together?

A CHINA MIÉVILLE —— I really disapprove of this question! It's a silver bullet question. Having said I disapprove of it, I think I have some good advice. I disagree with the typical advice that comes from writers 'write every day' and all of that – because one of the great problems for aspirational writers is the feeling that what you write should be read. It doesn't follow. We should start from the position that nothing we have written is worth reading. This doesn't mean that we shouldn't write it, only that you have to rigorously falsify that principle before putting it out there.

For all that I disapprove of the reduct‐ iveness of the question, I have some very reductive advice for anyone trying to write a novel. This is only really advice for people who haven't done it before, I should add. Firstly, turn off the internet. Beyond that I would recommend that you plan and plot in advance, because the notion that if you overplan something it will fall flat is utterly spurious. I think that is put forward too often by people who are unable to get beyond chapter two. It's not true, but even if it were, a flat chapter twenty is better than a non‐existent one.

An unwritten novel has a basilisk stare. It's just too big. The only way that most of us can write a novel is behind our own backs. The best way to do this is to focus on a day at a time. That doesn't mean just sit down and write, because then you end by rambling. What I think instead is that you should put aside a long time for really rigorous pre‐ planning. Just 'what happens, when'. Break it down chapter by chapter, down as low as you can, to 2,000-word chunks. First 2,000 words: 'Jane goes to the fridge and is attacked by a monster'. Second 2,000 words: 'The monster discusses Eliot,' you know, whatever the fuck. Plot it out so that you are going to be able to progress. Each day allow yourself a 1,000 words, so when you wake up on a Monday you know you have to get Jane from the bed halfway to the fridge, and you can forget all the other stuff. Forgetting about the novel is the best way of writing it.

BENJAMIN EASTHAM, SEPTEMBER 2012

WHAT KIND OF SPIDER UNDERSTANDS ARACHNAPHOBIA

BY

MATT CONNORS

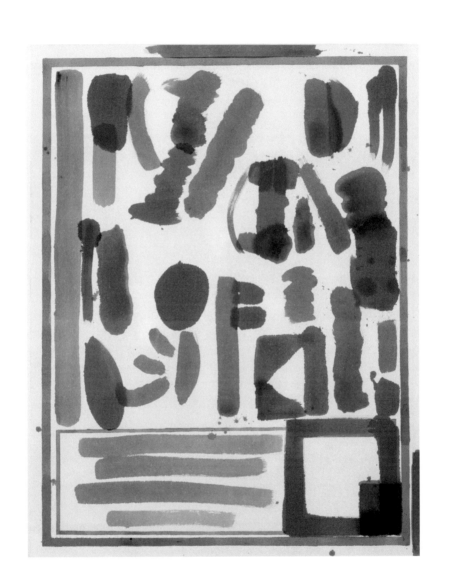

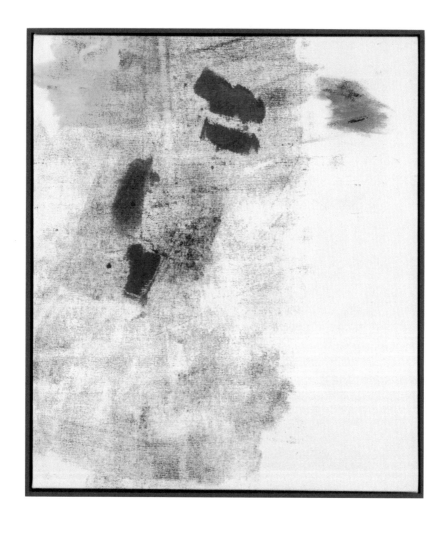

POEMS

BY

EMILY BERRY

OLIVIA MCCANNON

DAN O'BRIEN

TREES

They kept saying that my relationship history was so textbook.

Many of them were dissatisfied and they compared themselves to me and
they said that was what they wanted.

But the thing was I was dissatisfied too. I had my textbook relationship
history and that was okay, I was happy about that, but I had
other problems.

I don't want to mention them here because I don't always feel
comfortable telling people I don't know about my problems.

In general, despite my textbook relationship history and a few other life
successes I was fairly sure things were not going anywhere near as
well for me as they were for other people I knew.

I tried to rationalise this by saying to myself I bet that's what *they're*
thinking and who knows how they're *really* feeling.

Sometimes a friend would refer to someone we knew who seemed
happy and self-confident and successful in their career and
married and appeared to have no troubles whatsoever, and it was
very distressing.

If everything was really going so well for this person then how could we
explain our deep inner sadness?

Our own careers were going okay, so that helped. And of course I had my
textbook relationship history.

But on the other hand it didn't help, because if our careers had been going
badly and we had nobody to love us then perhaps our deep inner
sadness would have been justified.

There were also other matters, which seemed superficial, that bothered us.

For example, I had some nice furniture, but I was never satisfied with the
way it was arranged. Also, the colour of the curtains was too
similar to the colour of the upholstery. For god's sake, the colour
dominated the room.

I commented on this to my boyfriend a lot. Sometimes he was supportive
and went so far as to make suggestions and look online for
different armchair covers. Other times he just sighed angrily,
depending on his mood.

Also, I had a friend who was very concerned about the lowness of her
ceilings, even though, upon inspection, her ceilings were no lower
than anybody else's.

P

Was the problem hers, or was it ours, for having all come to accept an
        unconscionably low level of ceiling?
Did those who were happy and self-confident always reside in high-
        ceilinged homes?
I could give other examples.
Another friend, an academic, became irate once while denouncing
        psychoanalysis as a pseudo-science, and afterwards described the
        work of various other academics as 'gibberish'.
I wondered if 'gibberish' was just another kind of low ceiling.
How hard do you have to work to try to understand something before you
        can give up?
I had all these little theories about people I knew.
I exchanged them with other people for their theories and together we
        amassed huge banks of theories about people we knew.
It was some kind of leisure activity.
One of the jobs of these theories was to deflect attention from the agony
        of the self.
Another was to revel in it.
I could see three trees from my bedroom window: silver birch, willow, ash.
I looked out at them and thought of some of the things that troubled me:
        the kitchen's fruit fly population, the unravelling future, the
        unquantifiable nature of your pain versus my pain.
I looked out at them and said: 'I have been a student of myself for thirty-
        one years...'
I looked out at them and said: 'Is there anyone in the world who has
        written a cheque and not felt like they were playing the part of
        someone writing a cheque?'
I watched them quiver all over in a light breeze.

THE MUSCULARSKELETAL CONDITION

Every time I step outside I bang my soul on an osteopath.
When the phone rings it's usually an osteopath, calling to tell me
          about the new bones.
Osteopaths! I am tired of prostrating myself on your rolled-out
          strips of paper.
Sure, the muscularskeletal condition is just as important as the downturn!
It could be a contributing factor.
Yes, I will vote for you, osteopath.
I will praise your children.
I will consider holidaying in the Dordogne region.
Osteopaths, stop rummaging in my pockets I have nothing left.
Osteopaths, I'm sorry I didn't mean it.
It's just … the balance of power does not favour the achy.
(I can hear the coathangers jangling.)
Osteopaths, why are none of you in the government?
Osteopaths, how did you all meet and what do you talk about (besides
          the muscularskeletal condition) at the osteopaths' barbecues?
What would you do if everybody got better and you could no longer
          afford these premises?
Osteopaths, thank you for answering my questions.
Thank you for your sterile gel.
Thank you for your kind interest in my poetry.

'I SHARE YOUR DOUBT'

Hello. I share your doubt. I am full of uncertainty. I have a headache. I don't know anything. Inconclusive.

RUE DU FAUBOURG DU TEMPLE

The world in one road –
In it a SNACK with too many chairs
A fridge you might fall into up front
An Al-Jazeera window on the wall
Where a crowd in flames shakes fists
At the cervelle d'agneau you ordered

As the News made you nervous now
You must eat it you're twenty-five
This street these intervening lives
Wallpaper to your own sweet will
You step through apple tobacco fug
Into the stink of street-horn and shove

The pavement's a pitfall of spit and wheels
Dodge a baby's flung out arm　　now　　next
An oil-drum trolley hot with blackened corn
Men washed blue by strip-lit caves where
Teapots footballs phonecards proliferate or
Microwaves ping out soft pork dumplings

This will all never be anything but
The surface of what you'll never know
The vanishing forking wakes of flies
With troubled compasses stop-starting
Across the sheer skin that just holds
Over the depth of time and place.

P

CLOSURE

Open the door –

What did you expect? To find
The kitchen thick with bustle and steam
Smells – spitting egg – and exclamations
The football on small, crowds roaring
The garden beaming with beans, tomatoes
Poppies, bluetits, striped camping chairs,
Outhouse bright with affectionate washing
Its machines giddy-rocking and whirring
The kettle surging, the dark tea pouring?

The walls turn their back on you. Hard
Dead woodlice in piles of ten reckon up
The times that have not been passed here.
Cobwebs cordon off doorframes, the drop
Between each stair. Taps, cisterns, lav pans
Stand slack-jawed, with no-one to talk to
In that night-loud trickling tongue of theirs.
The chairs are awkward with the loneliness
Of not knowing who to belong to. You find

Indigestion tablets in a sewing tin, wedding
Rings in a matchbox. A house has its walls
That never change. A house has its boiler
That stays warm in its jacket for years. Here,
A pile of clothes on hangers, sorted, poised,
Not-in-the-end needed, is crumpling on a chair.
All that lived here has left. What this house was
You brought in with you. Take it out again.
The key sticks as you

Close the door.

THE WAR REPORTER PAUL WATSON
DESCRIBES THE GHOST

This is who you've always been. Your mind is
simply speaking to itself. You've become
the ghost. Is he here with us now? He is
always here, Herr Doktor. Like my shadow
in the sand. Standing sentinel, whispering,
This can not last. And of course he laments
whenever I lift the blade away from
my skin. I don't believe, you know, a ghost
could come walking through the door with a shroud
streaming clouds of what have you. I believe
there's a price to pay for this. The language
fails, but there's no escape. No matter what
religion, what culture, everyone knows
not to desecrate the dead. Not to look
except in horror or awe. That mob knew
exactly what they were doing. I pray
they're haunted like I am by the Afghan
looter aiming his mortar barrel at
my camera lens. *The truth is I'm afraid*
to meet you, Paul! You're the kind of writer
I've always wished I were. This mythical
figure with your hand, your constant return
to the underworld of that which we can't
look at, or won't look at. The Iraqi
looter's aiming his mortar barrel at
my laptop. *It's true he's gotten quieter*
now, I don't know why. Like he's waiting for
something, like a slasher movie. Maybe
my son will get leukaemia, or burn up
with my wife in a wreck. Who gives a shit
what happens to me! I know everyone
likes ghost stories, but it rarely works out
that way. You get used to it, it just turns
into someone else's problem.

P

THE WAR REPORTER PAUL WATSON
AT THE WIDOW'S HOUSE

Sunny Hill, Pristina. At a schoolhouse
where yesterday a boy got shot running
away. His body rots on his heels. Keep
back from the windows, this mother orders
her children, who are coughing and smearing
their noses on their coat sleeves. A neighbour
pressed his pistol into her daughter's rose
–bud cheek, Where is Baba? Before burning
their house to cinders. The classroom concrete
leaches the heat from your bones. So they lay
their heads on desks and slip out of focus
like psychopaths and slaves. *Can we help them
escape?* Either way it will be a sin,
you know. Stepping outside their mother shouts,
Do not make a sound! My translator is
asking zombies at cratered crossroads, Where
are the checkpoints now? Policemen's faces
absolved in balaclavas are seeking
justice. U–turns and dust plumes down side roads
till we find the widow's house. Who stands black
beneath her lintel. A shawl like a caul
over her sunken mouth. I can't even
help myself! she cries, peering through pissing
sleet at my idling Opel. I withdraw
some filthy bills. Driving away glimpsing
the youngest son's open palm slapping on
the window of the widow's house. *U-turns
and dust plumes down side roads.*

P

STOLEN LUCK

BY

HELEN DEWITT

KEITH WAS NOT THE SONGWRITER. Darren and Stewart wrote the songs. Keith hit things, some of which were drums. He came in one day with a song and nobody wanted to play it.

The song was the least of their problems. They had signed with a label, so their music was used in adverts and that, it brought in some dosh, they were shameless rock sluts because the fans downloaded the songs for free. Slutdom was not the issue. The issue was that the contract would not let them do independent gigs.

Keith had had an argument with them because the Arctic Monkeys, look at the fucking Arctic Monkeys, why the fuck can't we do what the fucking Arctic Monkeys, this being the capacity for inarticulate rage which had made him a drummer in the first

And Darren and Stewart, being songwriters, had talked and talked and talked and talked to the point that there were signatures on the contract.

Then the inconceivable had happened which is that Thom Yorke sent an email inviting them to do a gig. Keith said they should just do it, fuck the fucking contract but Darren and Stewart

So then Keith was very quiet.

Never a good sign.

Given Keith's known propensity to hit things other than drums.

So Darren said they would record the song.

Keith tried to explain his concept and Darren and Stewart kept arsing about and then Sean the keyboardist sussed that it was an arsing about session and then Keith put down his sticks.

Darren, Stewart and Sean sussed that the beat was gone.

Keith, says Darren. What the fuck.

Keith disengaged from the scaffolding of things that could be hit that made noise. He stood up.

He walked across the floor while Darren, Stewart and Sean varied the theme of What the fuck. He took the mic from Darren.

In addition to not being a songwriter Keith was not a singer. He dragged the lyrics of the song over reluctant vocal chords and spat them into the mic.

Fucking great man said Darren who did not want another guitar percussioned to subatomic particles against wall, floor, chair, his head. Yeah fucking great said Stewart who had also lost 3 guitars and Sean hastened to protect his keyboard from berserk drummer syndrome, Fucking great, insane, totally fucking crazy man

Keith handed the mic back to Darren. He turned and walked out the door.

F

The studio was in Limehouse. He walked west. His legs would not let him get on a bus.

At Leicester Square the crowd, wasn't there a director who gave every person in a crowd scene a thing to do? Sometimes the world is too convincing, as if someone spent too much time on it. Individualising the robots. He stopped at a corner.

On the pavement was this, like, guy with a sign beside him, CRAZY NICK AND HIS MUSICAL TRAFFIC CONES. There was an orange cone on the pavement beside him and he was holding another cone to his mouth, blowing into it. To the music of My Way.

pa PA, pa PA pa PA, pa PA pa PA, pa PA pa PA pa
pa PA, pa PA pa PA, pa PA pa PA, pa PA pa PA pa

People were dropping money in the cone. One woman, she put a ten pound note in the fucking cone.

PA   PA PA pa PA
pa PA pa PA
PA PA PA PA PA

He stood on the pavement.

pa pa
pa pa pa pa
pa pa pa ---- PAAAAAA PA

Like, fuck. A kid put 10p in the cone. The music was shite but here was this luckless tosser turning ostensibly irredeemable shite into gold with a simple traffic cone. Singlehandedly handling his own PR and marketing and sales and distribution. Say Thom Yorke comes upon the scene, says Hey, Crazy Nick, great act, OK if I join you, and Thom Yorke picks up the other traffic cone and does an impromptu gig with Crazy Nick—

Crazy Nick can say Yes, he can say Fuck off Radiohead wanker scum. Total artistic control.

He stood watching Crazy Nick for about 3 hours because

He walked east.

F

Marc was on the late shift at the News of the World. He wore a suit because hacks must dig for dirt in a suit. A call came in that a celeb was being a wanker in a pub, if swift action was taken photographic evidence might be shared with the British public, and Marc was the man for the job.

The celeb was Kyle Vaughan. He had a part in a soap. He stood by the bar with a rolled-up copy of the Big Issue, blowing My Way out of the orifice. Poop POOP poop POOP poop POOP poop POOP poop POOP poop POOP poop poop poop.

Not much value in it as a pic.

What I'm saying is, they're not doing enough to TRAIN, expatiated the celeb. Like, show some initiative, mate. You see them selling the Big Toilet Tissue and you want to say look, I have enough problems without constipating my brain with this crap, do something funny for a change, add value to the product

Marc: So you'd, like,

Like today I saw this bloke at Leicester Square, Crazy Nick and His Musical Traffic Cones, he's playing My Way on a traffic cone, I thought, you know, this just goes to show how fucking useless the Big Issue is, anyone with a little imagination can do more with a couple of fucking traffic cones

So you, did you give him some money, then? asked Marc.

Yeh. I gave him a quid. Which is what I'm saying.

Poop POOP poop POOP poop POOP poop POOP poop POOP poop POOP poop poop poop.

But maybe, maybe everyone can't be that innovative, do you think there's enough funny things that homeless people can do? Could you, like, do you have any ideas?

Yeh. Sure. Like. Like. Say you say to people, I am going to take my trousers off. If you pay me I will put them back on.

Yeh, maybe, said Marc, but see, maybe that's quite embarrassing, taking off your trousers in front of a lot of strangers, I mean, you wouldn't want to do it

Poop POOP poop POOP poop POOP poop POOP poop POOP poop POOP poop poop poop.

That's where you're wrong, mate. Because it's not about being a humung being it's about putting on a performance

Yeh but I don't see you doing it, easy to say, said Marc

And then it all happens very fast, the celeb is waving his Diesel jeans around his head and Marc is snapping pix and the celeb is shouting Wanker and Marc is heading for the door and the celeb is struggling to get into his Diesel jeans and Marc is in the street running

and he ducks into a doorway three swift corners down

and he gets out his phone and sends pix and they are dead chuffed, well done mate, they say and he walks under the cold sky on wet tarmac on which the bones of chickens and crumbs of fried batter mingle with dog turds, shiny crisp packets, a flattened Satsuma, he steps into the Oranges & Lemons & at the pinball machine is Keith O'Connor.

Marc orders a pint of Guinness. O'Connor is dancing with the pinball machine, pulling knobs, slapping the glass, leaning into it, pulling away. Marc sits on a plump leather bench. It's quiet.

The door opens. A bloke in a Tommy Hilfiger sweatshirt and Diesel jeans, bald, red face, goes to the bar, orders a Peroni, goes through swinging doors to a room behind the bar.

You all right, Tel.

Yeh. Yeh.

No offence mate but you look like shit.

Yeh. Well, me missus kicked me out.

Fuck.

Yeh— See, I was sitting at the end of the bar and this old geezer is talking to this girl and I say the word *cunt*. Not loud, like, but I do say it, but in a private conversation. So he hears me, and this is partly generational, he takes offence because his girl is there. So he says What did you say? So I don't want to make an issue of it, so I say All right, Stan, leave it, but he won't leave it alone, he says What did you say, so at this point I go over not meaning to do any serious damage but just to, you know, give him a little tap, but I misjudged the situation and broke his jaw.

Fuck.

Yeh. Yeh. This old geezer, and you know I would not normally hit someone that age Derek but he gave me no option, but then me missus says, You're not coming home.

Fuck.

Yeh.

Well, you can stay at mine or you can stay here. Frank and his lot are coming over after unloading, usual game.

It's been a long day.

The pinball machine is silent. Keith feeds it more coins. Marc occupies his suit.

Derek: In the north *cunt* is still an offensive word. You say that around somebody's girlfriend and he will exterminate you. In the south you hear it all over the place, people say Stop cunting me about, this sort of thing.

Tel: I'm all cunted out. I've heard that.

Derek: So stop cunting me about, you cunt, are you in or out.

Tel: Yeh all right then

Derek: You know what they say Tel, unlucky in love, this could just be your lucky night

F

Tel: Yeh. Yeh.

Teetleep Teetleep Teetleep Peep!

Teetleep Teetleep Teetleep Peep!

Beep! Beep!

Bebeep Beep Beep, Beep Beep Beep

Sorry, Tel, I think this is Frank — Frank, what the fuck, mate — yeh, yeh, sorry to hear that, Tel's here, yeh his missus was aggravated by an assault of Colonel Blimp or what have you so looks like Tel will be selling the Big Issue or something, yeh, help the homeless, so we on for tonight.

The pinball machine is silent. Marc is silent, nursing his foamy Guinness. Banter is tossed nonchalantly into the plastic mouthpiece, it is snatched from the air to burst forth at a distant earpiece, fresh banter pours into the waiting ear, it seems two of Frank's lot have been taken into custody, so if it's just the four of them including Tel maybe that is not enough to make it worthwhile, names of possible substitutes are proposed and rejected amid banter

Sorry, hold on Frank, yeh what is it?

Keith is standing at the bar. He wears a black t-shirt with a skeleton. His eyes are thickly mascaraed. There is glitter on his cheeks.

He says: You having a poker game?

Derek: We're talking about a friendly game among friends, mate.

Keith: This is how much money I have.

He takes a wallet from his back pocket and opens it, showing a thick soft pad of notes. This being the level of social savoir faire which led to Keith being a drummer in the

Derek: Yeh, well

Goes back on the phone with Frank.

Dunno, he says, bloke here might be up for it but I dunno, Frank, five, snot much of a game

But Marc is on his feet. This is KEITH O'CONNOR, drummer of the MISSING LYNX—

Marc is not into the pathos of semiotically enhanced footwear, is it a riposte to dualism that the intestines propel partially digested chicken tikka masala into the circumambient air when the eyes pass over the cover of a pb by Tony Parsons? What does it tell us of the human condition if the mind, pursuant to the expulsion of comestibles, explores the opposition between tearjerking & dickjerking — and yet somehow separate from the crap that now is Parsons is the history, the hack cavorting w/Johnny Rotten, this is a chance that will never

Words come to the plausible mouth.

I can play a bit, he says.

F

They are looking at the Suit, he should introduce the Suit separately, the estate of Lord Carnarvon had given his wardrobe to the Notting Hill Trust and now a garment that the body of a British aristocrat had worn to the House of Lords in 1953 (where it had excited no comment) had been handed into the keeping of a pleb for twenty quid to walk the world in low company.

And, like, Gerry! Maybe Gerry would like to play.

A sign above the door states that Gerald O'Hanlon is the proprietor licensed to sell intoxicating beverages.

Derek says: Don't be daft, Gerry's been up since 6am, last thing he wants is

Gerry says: You only live once.

He says: Look, Tel should not be on his own.

Marc scents: The money in the wallet, this is the thing they won't mention.

So it happens. Frank and the fortuitously uncustodised Maury are in their midst, Gerry locks up, there are seven men in a room behind swinging doors back of the bar.

They're playing Texas Hold 'em because that's what they've seen on TV.

For those who have not seen the game on TV: it's a doddle. Each player is dealt two cards. There's a round of betting. Three cards are dealt down the middle – the flop. A round of betting. A card is dealt – the turn. Another round of betting. A last card is dealt – the river. A final round of betting. Each player can combine any three of the cards on the table with the two in his hand to make up a 'poker hand'; the one with the best hand wins.

Marc has £51.63. The usual suspects are all buying chips for a friendly couple of hundred quid, which Marc reckons is to encourage Keith to do the same. Keith does buy in for a couple of hundred, which means Marc has to buy in for fifty quid. He does not expect to win; if he can walk away without losing more than five quid he'll count himself lucky. He's just trying to remember the ranking of hands as seen on TV.

Pair, two pair, three of a kind. Straight is five cards in numerical order. Flush is five cards of same suit, Flush beats a straight? Straight beats a flush? Full house is pair plus three of a kind. Four of a kind. Straight flush does what it says on the tin.

How many poker hands do you want to hear about?

You need to know about 3.

Marc started out with £50. On the third hand he picks up A K of spades. He bets 50p. Maury raises him £1. Frank sees the £1.50 and raises £1.50. Gerry sees the £3 and raises £3. Derek calls. Keith folds. Tel calls.

Marc thinks: Shit.

He calls.

Maury calls. Frank calls. The flop is King of diamonds Jack of diamonds 8 of spades. Marc checks. Maury bets £5. Frank folds. Gerry and Derek call.

Marc thinks: Shit.

He calls.

The turn is the 10 of spades. Marc bets £10. Maury calls. Gerry folds. Derek calls. The river is the Jack of spades. Marc bets £2. Maury raises him £10. Marc calls. Maury has Ace of diamonds Queen of diamonds. Marc wins £113.50.

It is obvious to everyone that Marc does not know what the fuck he is doing. Marc plays cautiously for the next 20 hands or so while Keith loses all his chips and buys in for another £300. There is much face-to-face banter.

Marc has inched his way up to £150. He would like to leave but he sits folding hand after hand. He picks up 8 9 of clubs. He is the big blind. He is in for 50p. Maury, Frank, Gerry, Tel and Keith stay in. The flop goes down and it is 10 7 of clubs J of spades.

Marc bets £2.

Maury raises £2. Frank, Gerry and Tel call. Keith raises £20.

Marc thinks: Shit.

He has seen the hands Keith has been betting on. He calls.

Maury, Frank, Gerry and Tel have seen the hands Keith has been betting on. They call. The turn is the 6 of clubs. Marc bets £5. Maury calls. Frank raises £10. Gerry folds. Tel calls. Keith raises £20. Marc calls. Maury folds. Frank calls. Tel folds.

The river goes down and it is the 9 of diamonds. Marc bets £10. Frank raises £20. Keith calls. Marc calls.

Frank has A K clubs. Keith has K Q of hearts.

Put Frank's hand with the board and you get A K 10 7 6 clubs. A flush. Which beats Keith's K Q (Hearts) plus J (Spades) 10 (Clubs) 9 (Diamonds). A straight.

After 3 hours Marc is totally confident that a flush beats a straight. So Keith is fucked. And under normal circumstances Frank's flush to the Ace would beat Marc's flush to the 10. But Marc, he checks again, yeah, he definitely has 10 9 8 7 6 of Clubs, which is a straight flush. So they are BOTH well and truly fucked by the King of the Hacks.

He thinks.

He hesitates to rake in the chips which he thinks are now rightfully his. There may be some arcane fact of poker lore such that if he shows he thinks he won he will look like a twat.

Derek says: I feel your pain, Frank.

Fucking A!!!!!!!!!!!!!!!!!!!!!!

As it says in the song, you don't count your money when you're sitting at the table. Basically Marc has won what is technically known as a shitload. He stacks the unexamined chips at his left.

F

Gerry says: I been up since 6, mates.

Tel says: You only live once, Ger.

Marc thinks: Shut. The fuck. Up. Just go to bed, you fucking wanker.

He thinks: But I don't have to

He's shivering. All he has to do is avoid fucking up and he can walk out with, like, 500 quid.

Marc does not feel he is really engaging with Keith, who seems to be in a chip-scattering bubble of solipsistic frenzy. He is not picking up anything NME-worthy. He feels like a twat in the Suit. It's also unbelievably boring. But if he can manage to survive the bollocks-withering tedium of the game he can

How many hands do you seriously want to hear about?

They play for another hour. Keith buys in for another £400. Marc tries to play unadventurously without looking like a cunt. Something in the ambience tells him he is not succeeding.

What happens.

Marc picks up 7 of diamonds 2 of clubs. He folds. Derek, Maury, Frank, Gerry, Tel and Keith stay in. The flop: A K Hearts 6 Spades. Derek is in for £5. Maury, Frank, Ger see him. Tel raises an unfriendly £50. Keith sees him and he is all in, which is to say that the wallet is now empty. There is an adjustment to the ambience. Marc gives it another 10 minutes before they pack it in and go home.

He can see them getting ready to fold, no point sending good money after bad, the hard faces with their pebble eyes assessing the exhaustion of the night's bounty.

Keith says: Look mate, I'll give you an IOU.

Ger says: No offence mate but cash only.

And Keith says: Look, I'm with a band. We've been signed and that. Four songs in the top 10. Missing Lynx.

Derek says: No offence mate but we would not take an IOU from Mick Jagger.

Meaning they have never fucking heard of the band.

And Marc in his 15 seconds of brain death says: Fucking fantastic band.

Keith turns to him. Maybe Marc is expecting to bond, as Tony Parsons allegedly did with Johnny Rotten and Joe Strummer and the giants of the past.

Keith says: Look, mate. I wrote a song. We recorded it today. If I assign the copyright to you, like, you can lend me 500 quid with the song as collateral.

Which is the way even a drummer can end up thinking and talking if he has spent quality time among the suits.

And the ambience adjusts yet again. Because now there is the possibility of transferring the dosh at Marc's elbow out of the safe custody of a hack who has been checking and folding all night, into the unsafe hands of a raving percussionist.

Go on then old cock, be a sport, says Frank, and Maury says, Least you can do, seeing as you're a fan and all, and Derek says, Got a piece of paper, Ger? And Ger says, Anything to help a friend,

and suddenly Keith is writing something on a cocktail napkin and signing it and telling Marc to sign and now Marc is sitting there with a cocktail napkin and Keith has many many many piles of chips.

Derek folds. The rest stay in, heartened by the influx of chips at the disposal of El Loco. The turn brings a 6 of hearts. Tel bets another unfriendly £50. Keith sees him. Frank sees him. Maury sees him. Ger folds. The last card goes down. It's the King of Spades. Tel bets £50. Keith raises £50. Frank and Maury fold. Tel raises £50. Keith goes all in, moving all Marc's former chips to the centre of the table. Tel sees him. Cards go down.

Keith has two Aces, making a full house.

Tel has two sixes.

Making 4 of a kind.

Keith says: Pa PA pa PA pa PA

pa PA pa PA pa PA

pa PA pa PA pa

Unlucky in love, Tel, says Derek. Remind me never to play with you again when yer missus kicks you out.

They're standing up, stretching, grumbling, talking about next week. It's over.

Tel is a grand ahead.

Keith has an empty wallet.

Marc has an autographed cocktail napkin.

Marc and Keith stand outside the Oranges and Lemons in the resentful London dawn.

Marc feels the severed 500 quid like an amputated limb. He's holding the cocktail napkin. It feels both worthless and, like, something he shouldn't have.

He says: Look, uh, Keith, you'd better have this back, I can't keep this.

Keith says: You can then. Not to worry, I'll pay you back. Gissa phone number.

Marc says: I'll show you mine if you'll show me yours.

He wants to say: This is not actually my suit. But this would involve explaining that he is a loathsome creature of Murdoch employ, perhaps insufficient exculpation.

He says: Uh, I'm actually a freelance journalist? Any chance I could, like, interview you sometime?

Keith looks at the Suit.

Styrofoam cups are trundling down the desolation of the Commercial Road under an indifferent breeze.

F

He says: Look. I want you to do me a favour.

Marc says: Yeah sure

Keith: You got whatever the fuck it is you wanted. So just wank off.

Marc: But

Keith: Just fucking Wank, the Fuck, Off.

Keith O'Connor is walking away.

The Suit knows how to deal with the situation. From a pocket comes a hand holding a camera.

*ZZZZZZZ*slik. *ZZZZZZZ*slik.

And for the fuck of it out of the practiced mouth comes: Hey KEITH!

And Keith O'Connor turns, slik slik slik slik

And Keith shouts: Wank OFF wank OFF you fucking wanker

And he turns again and he turns into a side street and Marc thinks: You stiffed me half a grand you wanker so who's the wanker

It's pretty quiet.

He puts the camera back in the convenient outside pocket. His hand touches something soft, the paper napkin. He transfers it to the inside pocket of Carnarvon's finest.

He can't use his last £1.63 on transportation, it has to see him to the end of the month. He trudges west.

At 7am Marc is in the Kingsway Starbucks recounting the evening's squalor to Lucy, who slips him a mega mocha latte and 3 blueberry muffins. He spends the next 5 hours rerererecounting to Claire at the Kingsway Caffè Nero, Nikki at the Holborn Pret a Manger, Eva at the Kingsway Costa Coffee, scoring much-needed provisions for the fundless month.

At noon the Evening Standard hauls in the punters with sorrowful news: KEITH O'CONNOR TRAGIC SUICIDE. He palms a discarded copy in the Shakespeare's Head and reads with shock and dismay.

But he is down to his last £1.63.

And he is on the phone to his minders at the News of the World with his scoop and they are dead chuffed, Well done mate, give us anything you got, and sure, Roger will be only too happy to reimburse the two hundred quid Marc allegedly lost in the game as a business expense, any pix, they would love to run a centre spread but they would love to have pix, well of course he has pix, what do you think? He has pix of Keith O'Connor's departing back heading down the desolation of the Commercial Road.

In this fashion did he honour Keith O'Connor's last request.

F

He did in fact write an in-depth analysis of the evening for NME.

Missing Lynx did in fact release the previously maligned song as a single. Which with tragic irony went straight to Number 5 in the charts and remained in the top 10 for an amazing 20 weeks.

Marc still has his cocktail napkin which still feels both worthless and like something he should not have. When the song has been at Number 5 for 6 weeks he sidles into the office of the lawyer at the Screws and brings the soft thing from the inside breast pocket of the aristocratic garment, anticipating that he will be dismissed as a twat for even contemplating the possibility that the relic of Oranges and Lemons revelry could be operational in a court of law.

    Gayatri says: Crikey. Well done you!

    She says: If they contest you might need witnesses, but as far as the language goes this is the business.

    We can reveal that Darren and Stewart had spent many hours analysing the source of Sting's wealth, which derives not least from the fact that he is the author of record of such classics as 'Every Breath You Take', 'Roxanne', 'Message in a Bottle', and 'Every Little Thing She Does is Magic', such that he receives a fee in the region of 12p (as of time of writing) every time said songs get air time, years or even decades after the songs slipped off the charts never to return. Whilst the other members of The Police get bugger all. The result being that Darren and Stewart had spent many hours arguing over credits for the songs of Missing Lynx, while Sean on keyboards and Keith on drums were never even conceivably going to be in a position to buy an island in the Caribbean. Such that Keith had lost valuable time that might have been spent hitting things absorbing the Language of the Suits by osmosis. Which stood him in good stead when he needed to transfer copyright to a song on a cocktail napkin.

So yeah, needless to say Darren and Stewart were not going to take this lying down, but Marc's newfound mates at the Oranges and Lemons rallied round, and Sean the keyboardist unexpectedly refused to remember that the song had been more of a thing they had all done together than something any one person could take credit for, and Marc was quids in.

    You can't always get what you want.

    Pa Pa Pa PAAAAAAAAAAAAA Pa.

INTERVIEW

WITH

EDMUND DE WAAL

AS WE SPEAK, EDMUND DE WAAL, CERAMICIST AND WRITER, MOVES HIS PALMS CONTINUALLY over the surface of the trestle table in his studio. He makes wide, flat waves in circular motions, as though he were smoothing it or wiping it clean. At times his hands curl into knots that knead the top of the wood. He is certainly emphatic – and there are tensions behind much of what he says; he is both strained by and earnest in his desire to make people actively 'look' at, not merely 'see' his work.

The publication in 2010 of *THE HARE WITH AMBER EYES* – his family memoir tracing the collection of 264 netsuke from *fin de siècle* Paris to the Palais Ephrussi in Vienna to Tokyo – propelled de Waal into the public eye. His renown as an artist is quieter though no less prestigious – he was appointed a Trustee of the V&A Museum and awarded an OBE for his services to art in 2011, and made a Senior Fellow at the Royal College of Art in June 2012. He has recently delivered lectures, participated in a panel discussion with Simon Schama and attended a screening of a film that documents the last year in his studio. De Waal insists that against all this activity and public engagement, his main sense of purpose derives from simply 'making things'.

De Waal has been making things since a pottery apprenticeship in 1981 with his tutor, Geoffrey Whiting, a pupil of the school of Bernard Leach. His education in ceramics continued in Japan and while his aesthetic remains sublimely simple, he has begun to create works with a more visible presence in the art world – such as *SIGNS & WONDERS*, a permanent piece installed in the atrium of the V&A in 2009. Forty metres above the entrance, 450 monochrome ceramics sit on a red lacquer shelf that runs the circumference of the ceiling dome, arranged in rhythmical groupings; each inspired by one of the museum's major ceramics collections. Of the work, de Waal says, 'It's not modest, but it's different.'

After we talk, he will visit his recent gallery show, *A THOUSAND HOURS*, at the Alan Cristea Gallery, for the last time before it closes. He has recently installed his first piece of public sculpture, a local history, at the new Alison Richard Building at the University of Cambridge. Future projects include an exhibition with the Chinese porcelain collections at the Fitzwilliam Museum in February 2013, more gallery shows and, of course, a new book.

———•———

Q. THE WHITE REVIEW — In a recent 'sermon' on the subject of tact you mentioned that you grew up listening to Leonard Cohen in a bedroom at the end of a hallway of medieval portraits. One can see a similar juxtaposition of styles – a reverence for antiquity against enigmatic and poetic pieces – in the installation of your work at Waddesdon Manor. You've called this setting an 'ersatz French chateau' and an 'extraordinary calling card' where 'everything is gilded'. How did you want people to experience your work in that space?

A. EDMUND DE WAAL — Almost everything to do with my pieces is about slowing down. Walking through that house, because of the wealth that surrounds you, you're eyeing everything very quickly and the way you actually move through rooms can be overwhelming. Amid the enchantment is the attempt to slow things down.

Q. THE WHITE REVIEW — To prompt visitors

to look in the crevices where they might not have done?

A. EDMUND DE WAAL — Yes. The act of 'looking' is absolutely about identifying all of the very peculiar, different types of spaces which you can use, because we have very conventional assumptions about where objects should sit. In the case of Waddesdon, it's very much about bringing your attention down or up or in, or around corners - to the surroundings.

Q. THE WHITE REVIEW — In *THE HARE WITH AMBER EYES*, you describe your inheritance from a Jewish banking dynasty, the Ephrussi family of financiers. The elaborate set-up at Waddesdon has parallels with the house on the Ringstraße in Vienna once owned by your family. Did you find yourself drawing similarities between what your pots were doing in certain rooms in Waddesdon and your imaginings, in the book, of the tiny details of your great-grandmother Emmy's dressing room in which the cabinet of netsuke was kept?

A. EDMUND DE WAAL — Yes, walking into Waddesdon Manor was absolutely like walking into the Palais Ephrussi, the two buildings are exactly the same date. The sheer amount of visual material, the abundance of gilded decoration, and the sense of one layer laid on top of another, it's absolutely the same. I was trying to *re*-occupy Waddesdon in a quite polemical way, but in a personal way as well.

Q. THE WHITE REVIEW — The Rothschild Collection at Waddesdon Manor comes from a tradition of members of the Jewish diaspora becoming prominent collectors of Dutch and French painting, and Sèvres pottery. Did it feel like a clichéd narrative to show there? Do you think that your ceramic works – quietly arresting because of the 'gilded' abundance in which they are inserted – perform a similar

role to that of the netsuke in the Palais?

A. EDMUND DE WAAL — Well, it was a dangerous kind of project because you don't want to make things which fit in too well, which feel too 'at home'. Otherwise it would become set dressing. It wasn't about that. It was much more about trying to identify places where you can interrogate particular ideas about collecting, such as boxes that can be packed up, things that you can see and not see, things that are scattered – like the five singular 'promises' – and one pair of vitrines in the Tower Room, called 'something else, somewhere other'.

I try to make things that are beautiful. I'm very open about that. The idea of something being site-specific, or site-sensitive, or being in conversation with its surroundings, is interesting, but you have to have the guts – you have to have enough chutzpah – to move away as well, to allow your installation to be of itself and not just disappear completely.

Q. THE WHITE REVIEW — Did you encourage distance?

A. EDMUND DE WAAL — Yes, but that's what vitrines do, if you do them well.

Q. THE WHITE REVIEW — In this contemporary art world, the very notion of the 'collector' has ambiguous connotations. How do you feel the role of the collector has changed? Take the example of Charles Ephrussi – your great-grandfather's cousin, a collector of works by Manet, Degas, Renoir, and Pissarro, and the inspiration for Charles Swann in Proust's *IN SEARCH OF LOST TIME* – he bought the entire collection of netsuke at once – he didn't build it up. Are there parallels that you see now?

A. EDMUND DE WAAL — The pathology of collecting is pretty much unchanged, I think. I don't see much difference in terms of collecting now – in terms of the enormous oligarchical creation of collections for ego, political power, national narrative, grandstanding, whatever. All those motivations were absolutely present in nineteenth-century collecting as well. The money's the same, the power's the same, the power relationships are the same, and the cultural prestige... they're all present still. I would be hard-pressed to find a different kind of *Belle Époque* collecting now. Sometimes it's visionary, sometimes it's sickening, and sometimes it's both at the same time. Collecting is at its heart an attempt to push mortality away by taking control of a part of the world. Collecting is the act of layering, of preservation, of building over and up. To collect is to take a bet on the future.

Q. THE WHITE REVIEW — You're an artist who collects. A work such as 'on the middle watch', displayed in your recent show at Alan Cristea Gallery, is a collection of pots: each piece is both independent and part of the whole. Do you consciously marry the concept of that act of amassing to the resultant 'whole'?

A. EDMUND DE WAAL — [Long silence.] No. What I see more clearly are the resultant gaps between the pots as they are arranged. I'm trying to make the spaces – the vacancies – more important. That's something that's become more important to me: the spaces *between* the objects or the spaces *around* the objects get bigger, or more complex. That's reflected in the fact that I am using opacity in my works, and vitrines, so that you can't see where objects lie. In that sense, what I'm doing is using the gaps and spaces and vacancies to heighten the awareness of the unknown. This absolutely mirrors my experience of reading, of vessels containing what is unsaid, or unwritten. Narrative is not just a pedestrian way of placing words one after another – and so

my pots don't sit in that kind of conjunction.

Q. THE WHITE REVIEW — There's a rather traditional view of ceramic work according to which the art is a modest one because it involves pots and plates – utilitarian objects. As a Daiwa Scholar studying at the Mejiro Ceramics Studio in Tokyo, you used the archives of Yanagi Soetsu. His theory was that such objects are beautiful precisely *because* they've been made in large numbers, chipping away at the notion of artistic ego.

A. EDMUND DE WAAL — It's complex stuff because that was the theory Bernard Leach – often honoured as the father of British studio pottery – took on, and that was my inheritance. The idea that the aim through repetition is to lose the ego is bullshit. It's a very controlling thing. But – and there is a huge 'but' – it is true that I experience an enormous freedom from having made 50,000 pots in my life. It's just like talking about [pianist] Mitsuko Uchida: every time she presses a key, the thousands of hours that she has put in are behind that! So, Yanagi is right, but his polemic is wrong. To moralise about it is wrong.

Q. THE WHITE REVIEW — Can you clarify the importance of Bernard Leach to your practice for those who are only coming to your work now? Your writings on Leach [de Waal's monograph on Leach was published by Tate Gallery Publishing in 1997] were deemed patricidal. Perhaps that's a melodramatic way of saying that you had simply moved on, but I am very interested in the idea that you have gone through ideological shifts and might yet go through others.

A. EDMUND DE WAAL — In a strange way, writing has enabled me to make a space in which to make things. Writing the Leach book allowed me to do something different; to make a different kind of pot. With my book on twentieth-century ceramics [published by Thames & Hudson in 2003], I was allowed to make some noise, which was great, and *THE HARE WITH AMBER EYES* allowed me to be private in public. I am writing a new book, and there is a weird symbiosis between saying something in words and my practice; they weave together. There are these moments of ideological rupture – the Leach book was *incredibly* liberating.

Q. THE WHITE REVIEW —— You said in your speech at The School of Life that 'the non-declamatory has a particular kind of power', and I would suggest that's what Leach dictated. He didn't allow anyone to make any declarations. Pottery was merely of use, and one must be austere in refusing to give these objects importance beyond their utility. Do you return to Leach often, and do you continue to reject him?

A. EDMUND DE WAAL —— No, I don't. It's not outright rejection because I still think about my connection to different kinds of tradition. The problem for me – and why I still find Leach both interesting and annoying – is that his rhetoric was so *totalling*. His rhetorical position around pots was so wrong, and he did tell people what to do. As someone who talks about pots, I say that it's all possible. It's an attempt to open up the practice.

Q. THE WHITE REVIEW —— One could draw a family tree between figures like Leach and Geoffrey Whiting, your tutor at King's School, Canterbury and a disciple of Leach, but also the movements from which you've inherited ideas in some form or another, such as the Arts & Crafts movement, parts of the Bauhaus, the Wiener Werkstätte...

A. EDMUND DE WAAL —— It's a bit like *THE*

ANXIETY OF INFLUENCE: choose your oppressor well. I'm reluctant to mention Harold Bloom, but he's absolutely right on the point of whom you choose to be made anxious by, and how productive your anxiety proves. It's been very useful for me.

Q. THE WHITE REVIEW —— I don't think people have quite mentioned – in great volume, at least – the influence of minimalism on your work. You tried to condition that term in conversation with Simon Schama recently. He said there's a type of 'exquisite' minimalism to your work because it is so attuned to the senses, or any kind of veiled emotion or human feeling.

A. EDMUND DE WAAL —— In my dreams.

Q. THE WHITE REVIEW —— Well, you discussed still lives as a form of exquisite minimalism – on just one visual plane you have all the power – the punch – of a very *pure* point.

A. EDMUND DE WAAL —— I do believe in a kind of sensuous minimalism which is conceptually really sorted, and is as rigorous as any pure, bloody, terrifying late sixties minimalist figure like Donald Judd. This is also a minimalism that has real emotion in it. And Agnes Martin knows that sense of poetic minimalism, which works for me.

Q. THE WHITE REVIEW —— So many of your works' titles derive from poetry. Is that a con-scious attempt to veer away from anonymity, the numerical, or the automatic?

A. EDMUND DE WAAL —— Oh, like 'Objecthood #7'. Yes, the relationship between poetry and objects has always been there for me. It's just that it took a long time before I felt allowed to say that in public. Actually, they *are* poems. They look like stanzas. To me, objects and words are very much the same thing. The word is an object. Meanwhile, the naming of the works has come quite late in my career – only in the last ten years. It was a threshold for me to say 'You know what? I just don't care any more. They are poems. And this is the title of the poem.' And it was alright!

Q. THE WHITE REVIEW — Your first vitrine, for the 2010 show FROM ZERO at Alan Cristea Gallery, was a piece in which you had central pots surrounded by marginalia, paralleling a medieval manuscript with notations clustering around a central text. However, you created another vitrine with an opaque glass surface. Were you aiming to hold the first one back?
A. EDMUND DE WAAL — Yes, exactly. It felt too abrupt and it just needed protecting. Of course, when there are two vitrines together, they would be closed – like pages in a book. I hear and read the world through words, and see words constantly, as well as rhythms and objects. Words are incredibly present for me on any surface. Look, [points to a shelf] there's some butter, some sugar and some keys. When I see that, it's a visual experience but I also *hear* it as words. The question for me is: what am I putting out in the world? Am I writing, or am I making? I'm doing both.

Q. THE WHITE REVIEW — *THE HARE WITH AMBER EYES* is a very visual work. The experience of reading it is very much one of looking. But you've increasingly brought the effect of blurriness into your work. If I were a psychoanalyst, I would say that you're protecting yourself against the growing media glare.
A. EDMUND DE WAAL — You're right. There's a sense of self-protection but it is also not melancholic, or vague. I'm not trying to be annoying or postmodern with the opaque or translucent vitrine surfaces. It's much more important to me than that. It's an odd thing, but sometimes the things that I've looked at hard

enough and repeatedly show blurred qualities. They hold a very strong place within memory, and they are very intense. Indeed, in poetry, lines become so intense and so precious that I can hold them. It's so precious that I don't want to look at it in an abrupt way. I can, of course, take it out and remember it and appreciate it, but in my memory it's got the protective blur around it.

Q. THE WHITE REVIEW — Does that desire to return to objects make permanent installations, such as the recent one you've done in Cambridge, or *SIGNS & WONDERS* at the V&A, more attractive to you as an artist? Would you like to continue to create public works of art?
A. EDMUND DE WAAL — Yes, I'd love to. The thing to be really wary of is their permanence, and that each commission needs a different approach. There are people who install public works of art that have an overblown quality, stating that they're here forever. It can be very egotistical. I like the idea of having something that takes up a bit of space that no one knew about – like the installation at the V&A.

Q. THE WHITE REVIEW — You have described how porcelain was known in the eighteenth century as 'white gold' – partly due to its value and partly because of its relationship to alchemy – and how gold was used to repair broken porcelain.
A. EDMUND DE WAAL — My new book takes porcelain as its narrative thread. It's about how difficult, and how necessary, it is to make something that is *white* in this world. The obsession with frailty and death, with the precious, the clean. This pure whiteness connects to extreme emotions or states, and I talk about the human cost of these pots being made. It's absolutely about people. I'm interested in the unwritten histories of how

objects are made.

I went to Dublin on a research trip to see the Fonthill Vase, the most famous bit of porcelain in the West. It was made in 1300 in China, and was in the possession of the King of Hungary in 1310, and then the Duc de Berry, and the dauphin, and it went through all these places, on these very beautiful early Renaissance silver mounts. It ended up in the National Museum of Ireland, so I went to spend an afternoon with it.

Q. THE WHITE REVIEW —— It makes me think how much an object can *hold*, how much it can bear, having been held by so many people.
A. EDMUND DE WAAL —— Yes, it's a good example, because this hasn't been picked up for twenty-five years, it's remained in a glass case. You pick it up and see its fire mark, so you know the person who made it – the people who made it – in Jingdezhen. You feel the weight, you feel what the people who made it felt, and you see that where something went wrong, they thought it was good enough to go, the decoration that happened, and you're away. Petrarch would have seen it. It would have been at court with the Duc de Berry along with the *TRÈS RICHES HEURES*, in the same rooms as the great medieval wall tapestries. It survived the French Revolution in a particularly extraordinary way, and then it was lost, and later was looted by the Nazis... And I can pick it up and I know where the clay came from because in July I walked up a mountain to find that place, just outside Jingdezhen, the city of porcelain. I was able to spend time sitting with those in Jingdezhen who still make the tiny little porcelain flowers that go on ceramics.

This is all to say that I am tracing the history of white, and porcelain, but it's a real story. It's about the capacity of objects to carry and to resist at the same time. It's about going back, going back, going back, as far as you can, and then back even further...

Q. THE WHITE REVIEW —— Is the book finished?
A. EDMUND DE WAAL —— It's not fully formed yet. With writing, it's hard to ascertain what is foreground and what is background early on. The book also explores *MOBY DICK*, Agnes Martin, Goethe's writing on colour... By the way, I resist the term 'biography' – in this case of a colour – as it was applied to my last book.

Q. THE WHITE REVIEW —— Alongside performative lectures and talks, you've written on Cy Twombly for Gagosian Gallery and mentioned that he's a hero of yours. Will you keep on writing about your influences?
A. EDMUND DE WAAL —— I'm actually trying not to write! I'm trying not to do more talking, I'm trying not to do more writing, to just put my energy into writing the book and my forthcoming shows and projects. Sometimes these smaller pieces of writing are productive distractions, but they are distractions. The core things I do are making things and producing pieces of sustained writing. There are so many pressures of being out in the world – during an exhibition, you're supposed to do things which help people to 'understand' your show – and if you're writing a book... well, there's stuff around that too, so it's a question of trying to keep everything alive.

Q. THE WHITE REVIEW —— You do a remarkable job of it. At a recent talk you were asked how you felt about people not being able to touch your pots – your reaction suggested it was an egregious question.
A. EDMUND DE WAAL —— It was a slightly egregious question, but understandable . What I want to do is to make work that has a place in

the world – and that's not about picking it up. Just because I wrote that bloody book doesn't mean I have to be the flag–waver for tactility and the power of touch. I don't have to do that. I'm so excited by the power of *not* touching. Telling artists what to do is like telling writers what to write: 'You're a potter, so why am I not allowed to pick it up anymore?' I mean, fuck off! It is what it is. You might not *like* it, but to touch something is not a right. It's the act of understanding how objects work in the world. There's a different kind of tuning in that develops with looking rather than touching.

Q. THE WHITE REVIEW —— Colm Tóibín provided a short story, 'The Arrangement', for your recent exhibition catalogue. Writing in the style of Joseph Conrad, he conjures the atmosphere of being on a ship in search of something, waiting. He starts with the line, 'At this distance I am still clear about most of the details.' His last line: 'If I had the patience, it would come about. All we both had to do now was watch.' Anticipation is central to your work. Everything is couched in a sense of hiddenness which only slowly is revealed – it's a process in time.

A. EDMUND DE WAAL —— I hope so. That's longevity. There are some things that stay with you. And some just fall away, because they haven't got the space for you to grow into.

EMMELINE FRANCIS, NOVEMBER 2012

THE AGE OF BRASS

BY

HUGH FOLEY

DELIVERING A SPEECH AT CAMBRIDGE UNIVERSITY in November
2011 on 'The Idea of a University', Higher Education Minister David Willets was
interrupted by shouts from the lecture hall. Rather than employing such tried and
tested heckles as 'Tory scum!', the audience declaimed a call-and-response poem.
There are not many places poetry would be considered the natural response to an
assault on higher education, but in Cambridge the notion of resisting capitalism
through verse has an illustrious tradition. The student identified as the group's leader,
Owen Holland, a Ph.D. candidate in English, was 'rusticated' for seven terms. One
of the many outraged responses to this verdict (leading to its eventual reduction to
a single term) argued that a protest must be able to 'uncover the gross disparities of
authority and intimidation that lie below the skin of reasonableness'. The author of
this sentiment is a man central to Cambridge's tradition of poetic dissent, and a poet
whose own work sees beneath the skin of reasonableness – Jeremy Halvard Prynne,
J. H. to his readers.

    Born in 1936, Prynne is a Life Fellow in English at Gonville and Caius College,
Cambridge. He was also, until recently, its librarian. Unlike his fellow university
librarian Philip Larkin, Prynne writes poetry that, at first glance, is neither readily
accessible nor closely tied to the traditional forms of English verse. The presence of
a recognisable human voice is hard to establish, as are coherent settings or narratives
and the politics, where they can be deciphered, are radical. These tendencies, along
with his typical refusal to publish works through the regular channels, tend to place
Prynne low down in the odds for poetry prizes. Ushered into the press mainly to be
attacked for being incomprehensible, or occasionally politely dismissed for not being
'generous' to the reader, it might seem that Prynne will remain in the library, never
able to enter the wider British consciousness in a manner comparable to Larkin.

    Despite his relative obscurity, Prynne is as central as Larkin to any reckoning of
the poetry written in Britain in the last fifty years. It is not just his own impressive
body of work; it is also what he represents to other poets. If one were to draw, very
crudely, the battle lines that still divide much contemporary British poetry, the two
sides might be said to line up behind Larkin or Prynne. It is not so much that all poets
sound like one or the other, but that each can be seen as the embodiment of certain
tendencies. Prynne and the 'Cambridge School' of poets that developed alongside him,
and then under his watchful eye, represent the most enduring aspect of a British
radical modernist tradition.

¶ Prynne is one of a generation of poets that came of age after the Movement, the
anti-modernist backlash that dominated the English fifties. The Movement poets –
Larkin, Kingsley Amis, Elizabeth Jennings, Thom Gunn (later an apostate), Robert
Conquest, John Wain and (more complicatedly) Donald Davie, who taught Prynne

at Cambridge, sought to push back against modernism. Prynne, alongside the likes of Ted Hughes and Geoffrey Hill rejected this anti-modernist consensus, which Al Alvarez called the 'gentility principle' in his introduction to THE NEW POETRY, criticising the Movement poets even as he anthologised them. Where Hughes adopted a muscular free verse and Hill embraced the allusive and hieratic, Prynne was driven to break with the period style by contact with the wild fringes of American poetry.

This came first through the Cambridge-based PROSPECT magazine, started by Elaine Feinstein, and through contact with Ed Dorn, an American who brought with him entirely new ideas about poetry and put him in touch with Charles Olson. The eccentric Olson had been rector of the influential, unorthodox Black Mountain College, the liberal arts institution at which John Cage, Merce Cunningham, Buckminster Fuller and Robert Motherwell taught during the post-war period. As well as Dorn and Olson, poets such as Robert Duncan, Robert Creeley and Denise Levertov all passed through. In the sixties Olson was working on his magnum opus, THE MAXIMUS POEMS, an epic about Gloucester, Massachusetts, where he lived. The poet's historical and even geological concern found a chime in Prynne, whose poetry also places humanity against large scales. It is Olson's influence, more than that of any other American, which can be heard in early Prynne:

> even the night is drummed
> by whippoorwills, and we get
>
> as busy, we plow, we move,
> we break out, we love. The secret
>
> which got lost neither hides
> nor reveals itself, it shows forth
>
> tokens. And we rush
> to catch up.

This is from Olson's 'Variations done for Gerald Van de Wiele', and we can recognise similarities of tone in Prynne's 'In Cimmerian Darkness':

> When the faint star does take
> us into the deeper parts
> of the night there is
> that sudden dip
> and we swing across into

E

> some other version of this
>
> present age, where any curving
>
> trust is set into
>
> the nature of man, the green raw and fabulous
>
> love of it, where every star that shines,
>
> as he said, exists
>
> in love…

The collection from which this poem is taken, *THE WHITE STONES*, often marks the last point that sceptics allow Prynne's poetry to have any value at all. Soon Prynne would shift away from Olson: humanity is already much less the subject of Prynne's verbs than Olson's. It is not part of the process, but subject to it in another sense. Where Olson conceived purging poetry of 'lyrical interference from the individual as ego' as a kind of heroic pursuit, the individual for Prynne is far less capable of self–transcendence.

Prynne instead made a radical move. This being the age of Vietnam and the New Left, it seemed inadequate to use poetry as a projection of egoless unity with the world. Prynne's poetry from this period begins insisting on the existence of oppressive forces at ever more fundamental levels of language use. Concepts such as the self become problematic in this kind of poetry, not as 'interference' but as pernicious fictions. They deny a real encounter with the social forces that determine every aspect of one's experience. A 'Cimmerian Darkness', Prynne goes on to show, is not the same as empty space.

1972's *BRASS* marks the point at which Prynne's war against residual 'naïve' lyricism begins in earnest, proffering a resistant language that refuses to make the world palatable. The opening poem at first sounds like early Prynne, 'Gradually they evade the halflight / rising for me, on the frosty abyss', but soon mocks itself, 'Thereby take / the foretaste of a style'. From here the language becomes increasingly interruptive; specialist vocabulary bursts into passages and the reader is directed to think on a larger scale than that of personal epiphany. This is the close of 'Rich In Vitamin C', one of Prynne's finest shorter poems:

> You come in
> by the same door, you carry
>
> what cannot be left for its own
> sweet shimmer of reason, its false blood;
> the same tint I hear with the pulse it touches
> and will not melt. Such shading

of the rose to its stock tips the bolt
from the sky, rising in its effect of what
motto we call peace talks. And yes the
quiet turn of your page is the day
tilting so, faded in the light.

Prynne may have rejected standard tropes of lyricism and beauty, but that doesn't mean he doesn't know how to deploy them. This stanza is simultaneously puzzling and alluringly pretty. Roses, bolts from the sky and fading light aren't put to anything like their usual employments. Every word is made to sweat out its multiple meanings. The lines 'such shading/of the rose to its stock tips the bolt' propose art as something that creates illusion by 'shading' the rose. The implication of art in commercialisation is suggested by 'stock tips' – roses reduced to commodity – before the full syntax reveals shading the rose to its stock tipping the bolt. The rose is drawn with the stock of a bolt action rifle, elsewhere in the poem gestured to by the 'herbal jolt of Cordite', a propellant that replaced gunpowder and was itself replaced in the development of modern warfare. For Prynne as for William Carlos Williams 'The rose is obsolete', a 'stock' phrase or 'stock' character, but Prynne wants us to think about the role poems about roses play as carriers of violent and violently commercial ideology. Poems are 'peace talks' reduced to 'mottos' (always a kind of advertisement like 'Don't be evil'), themselves subordinated to an 'effect' of guns. For Prynne, the originary acts of violence that create social order cannot but colour a poem. Perhaps the 'day … faded in the light' is the diminished sense of beauty when this complicity is revealed.

Prynne's focus since the beginning of the seventies has been to integrate into the poetic moment the vast and structural injustices it normally excludes. To do this, he incorporates an enormous vocabulary, encompassing hundreds of specialist disciplines. Take *HIGH PINK ON CHROME* (1975): this sequence is a Wordsworthian exploration of man's place in nature, constantly interrupted by the language of agri-business. The title evokes the romantic sunrise or sunset over metal silos, while the poem opens:

Pink star of the languid
Settles by a low window
Lap to flit, give the life
Too quickly, the storm
A mere levelled gaze.

Even this ambivalent depiction of a sunset is soon replaced by lines like 'he farms the pelt with aniline' or reminders that 'pork chops are up again'. Hear the voice of the bard, who past, present and commodity futures sees.

> In feare and trembling they descend
> Into threatened shock. Faire and
> Softly, too far from the dry arbour.
> The chisel plough meets tough going,
> We spray off with paraquat 2 1/2 pints
> Per acre. And the 51cr label shews
> Them and us in your same little boat,

Paraquat is a weed killer, which thirty–two years after this poem was written was banned in the EU. 51cr is a radioisotope of chromium, and chromium compounds, such as the ones used in tanning leather, are pollutants. The 'same boat' we're in is the skin of the slaughtered animals, whose pelts were earlier tanned 'with aniline'. The velar consonantal chime of 'acre' and '51cr' show the shifts both in the language and the chemical composition of the land. Poetry is not subject here to value judgements premised upon aesthetic sensibility: all is poetry, from factory farming to the conditions of modern warfare.

T. S. Eliot proposed a theory of poetic consciousness in his essay 'The Metaphysical Poets' that, although now unfashionable, held considerable sway around the time that Prynne began university. For Eliot, after the English Civil War, poets began to exhibit what he called a 'dissociation of sensibility'. The difference between a whole and a dissociated sensibility was that

> A thought to Donne was an experience; it modified his sensibility. When a poet's mind
> is perfectly equipped for its work, it is constantly amalgamating disparate experience;
> the ordinary man's experience is chaotic, irregular, fragmentary. The latter falls in love,
> or reads Spinoza, and these two experiences have nothing to do with each other.

Prynne's poetry effects a Marxist twist on this thought. Few poets, few people, understand recent developments in quantum physics, but fewer still attempt to incorporate these ideas into an interrogation of what it means to live under late capitalism. Prynne may not be able to overcome the division of mental from manual labour, but he seems to want to do something about the fragmenting specialisation of thought work. Considering the scale of this enterprise, far beyond any notions of the 'common reader', it may result in a poetry that at first seems aggressively recondite. It is an irony of history that Britain's most disjunctive poet is perhaps the one with its least dissociated sensibility.

When I. A. Richards, the inventor of 'practical criticism', founded the English

E

department at Cambridge he asked Eliot to join him. Though Eliot declined, his writings were treated there like holy writ. Jeremy Noel-Tod, writing in the *CAMBRIDGE LITERARY REVIEW*, has already identified the close ties between the theorising of modernist poetry in English and Cambridge academia. Prynne himself is the author of tips for Practical Criticism for new Caius students and continues, in his own fashion, the tradition not bequeathed so much as triggered by the author of 'The Waste Land'.

It is a particularly British form of literary theory, a tradition encompassing F. R. Leavis and William Empson, which perceives a moral value in the form by which poetry attempts to grasp the world. This academic tradition marks the difference between what came to be called the Cambridge School and other British 'alternative' groupings, like the London groups around Bob Cobbing, Barry MacSweeney or Eric Mottram. There are plenty of other poets in academia (such as Mottram himself), but few work as hard to unite the two pursuits. Prynne is a dedicated philologist, his only published critical books being commentaries on individual poems, one of which, on Shakespeare's 'Sonnet 94', explores the etymology of every word in the poem. Prynne's poems don't have notes, they have references.

A host of poets have issued forth from Cambridge in this tradition. Even before Prynne's identification as the North Star of underground poetry the Cambridge scene was important. There were Peter Riley and Andrew Crozier, the younger philosopher–poet Denise Riley (one of comparatively few women and no relation to Peter). Outside the university, there were Tom Raworth and Douglas Oliver. There was also Prynne's fellow student at Caius and close friend, the late R. F. Langley, who published very little poetry in his lifetime and deviated considerably from the norms of what would later become known as the Cambridge School.

Aspiring poets continue to be captivated by the lecturer whose commitment to difficulty has made him a cult figure, and by the poetic world around him. There are Veronica Forrest-Thompson, who died too early, Andrew Duncan, John Wilkinson, Drew Milne, Simon Jarvis, Keston Sutherland, Andrea Brady, Justin Katko, Emily Critchley (whose relationship to the Cambridge School is more complicated, and seems less directly Prynnian) and more to come. Cambridge remains the town to do business for 'linguistically innovative' poets. These poets have helped to construct a parallel world from what is still called the mainstream, for which Faber and Faber seems to serve as metonym. That publishing house, perhaps ironically considering its close affiliation with Eliot, is frequently held up as a straw man to be beaten for naïvety, quietism, banality or worse. For many years the university hosted the waggishly titled Cambridge Conference of Contemporary Poetry (CCCP), presumably opposed to the National Society for Direct, Accessible Poetry, providing a base for attacks against conservatism, political or poetic.

Though their poetry differs from Prynne's and each other's significantly (Simon

E

Jarvis's THE UNCONDITIONAL, for example, is written mostly in iambic pentameter), these poets can be seen to share certain positions on the relationship between language and politics. There is a consistent concern that the reader be able to infer the world's structural injustices, and a resistance to them, from close attention to a poem's form. Whether they are justified in their accusations that most mainstream poems are naïve (or cynical) in ignoring those injustices, the concern manifests itself in a prevailing opposition to unified speakers, normative syntax and decorative metaphor. It is by their opposition to prevailing linguistic modes that we might distinguish these poets from their peers.

These differences incite some strident opposition. The Scottish poet Don Paterson opines that 'the Norwich phone book or a set of log tables would serve [readers] as well as their Prynne', while Craig Raine dismisses Prynne as 'emulatively difficult'. When Prynne was trumpeted as Britain's most important living poet in Randall Stevenson's OXFORD COMPANION TO TWENTIETH CENTURY BRITISH AND IRISH POETRY, the claim drew puzzlement or vituperation. The mainstream papers rushed to ask 'Who is Jeremy Prynne?' and 'What is he on about?', while some poets scathingly replied that no one knew. This could be interpreted as defensiveness. By gearing for posterity in the way Joyce suggested – 'keep the professors busy' – Prynne and his acolytes might yet muscle the mainstream out of the canon. Given the chance to determine it, they would indeed throw much recent British poetry out.

In his essay 'The Trade in Bathos', Keston Sutherland makes the clearest statement of this antipathy. He has brought recent Cambridge poetry and these impulses, if not into the popular consciousness, at least into some of what passes for the limelight in poetry. He is among the most interesting and visible of the poets influenced by Prynne, and as the editor of Prynne's forthcoming COLLECTED PROSE is often thought of as his anointed successor. Thanks to him, another bastion of poetic radicalism has been established at the University of Sussex, producing the likes of Joe Luna and Francesca Lisette.

Sutherland's poetry takes a different approach to the same problem as Prynne's, just as his visible presence and dramatic performances contrast starkly with Prynne's reluctance to take to a stage. In the latter's late work, the position of personality is at once almost utterly determined and impossible to transcend, 'petrol in search of flame hardly a ham sand/wich'. American poets of a comparably experimental bent, like the L=A=N=G=U=A=G=E poets, tend to think of a deconstruction of the 'subject' as somehow liberating, giving the reader the freedom to create their own meaning. To Prynne this is merely 'the classic freedom to eat cake', and a denial of the possibility of an agency capable of effecting real changes. If Prynne seems to be granting less and less power to that agency as his work goes on, Sutherland's poetry at least appears to desire it.

E

The linguistically innovative British poets share with the hippie-ish British Poetry Revival that preceded them an oscillation between the professorial and the adolescent. Theory-speak and the word 'fuck' are rarely far removed. Sutherland's major works seem to embrace adolescence as a productive position, making an argument for it as the most intensely lived form of experience under capitalism. From rock and roll to fashion, adolescent choices are motivated by the desire to rebel against a stultifying system by consuming more of what sustains it. The viciousness of the double bind that Prynne shows in his dissections of poetic language can also be seen in the teenager who storms out from his bourgeois family to hang out in the mall. Take the opening of HOT WHITE ANDY:

> Lavrov and the Stock Wizard levitate over to
> the blackened dogmatic catwalk and you eat them. Now swap
> *buy* for *eat*, then *fuck* for *buy*, then *ruminate* for *fuck*,
> phlegmophrenic, want to go to the windfarm,
> *Your* · kids menu lips swinging in the Cathex-Wizzmonoplex;
> *Your* · face lifting triple its age in Wuhan die-cut peel lids

Eating, buying and fucking have become interchangeable acts of consumption, as has thought; 'ruminate' posits a cow's chewing as cogitation. The 'blackened dogmatic catwalk' may be an image of the wreckage of history, but it is also a very teenaged one, a place to strike a pose. Soon the sense of being denied adult agency, so common to adolescence, becomes exaggerated to the point of childishness: 'want to go to the windfarm', the poet says in mock petulance.

Those on the radical Left who demand a better world are often accused of childishness, and it is interesting to see him address this accusation. Sutherland's poem wants to grow up into real love, even as it reveals its childishness. This can be seen again in his ODES TO TL61P (an obsolete Hotpoint dryer), which interweaves some version of the poet's adolescent sexual history into an attempt to think outside the limitations of contemporary capitalism. Sutherland's poetry gains power from the frustration of desire. Towards the end of HOT WHITE ANDY, the poem informs us that 'the superpower to come is love itself', in which it is hard not to read Larkin's 'what will survive of us is love'. The line might owe more to early Prynne lines like 'born at long last into the image of love', but it's nice to attempt a doomed reconciliation occasionally.

There is a dangerous aspect to this poetry. A large part of its power comes from the giddy distance between the exploited and those who live by their exploitation (among them Western poets). This becomes the sublime object contemplated. Is it enough if someone writes, as Sutherland does, in order to change the world? Perhaps not, but it

E

is something. If poetry is about honesty then it must be honest about our implication in unjust systems. Much of the most important British poetry written in response to the Iraq War came from those poets associated with Prynne. REFUSE COLLECTION was Prynne's response to the abuses in occupied Iraq, as were Sutherland's STRESS POSITION and Andrea Brady's EMBRACE. Rather than establishing an artificial distance between poet and the actions of the state, the resistant language establishes a position for the poet to write an honest critique that acknowledges rather than evades complicity.

This may be the most important legacy of J. H. Prynne. The constant blockage and resistance of his late verse, as if words were magnets stuck together at the wrong ends, can produce a breakdown of reading. A kind of exhausted despair may not be the only feeling one wants from poetry but it is not complacent. You don't have to agree with all aspects of Prynne's project to respect the strength of feeling that drives a man to speak in a way that might make him hard to listen to. It might be that the domestic lyric is not always the worst act of false consciousness. It might be that we are entitled to the consolations of poetic moments that we experience as outside of politics (even if they are not). Maybe there are other legitimate and honest ways of responding to our position in the world, but these are not adequate reasons to dismiss Prynne's achievement.

In THE FOUR AGES OF POETRY, the nineteenth-century writer Thomas Love Peacock argued that the final age of poetry was the 'Age of Brass', an age in which:

> mathematicians, astronomers, chemists, moralists, metaphysicians, historians, politic-
> ians, and political economists, who have built into the upper air of intelligence a
> pyramid, from the summit of which they see the modern Parnassus far beneath
> them, and, knowing how small a place it occupies in the comprehensiveness of their
> prospect, smile at the little ambition and the circumscribed perceptions with which the
> drivellers and mountebanks upon it are contending for the poetical palm.

This tongue-in-cheek riff on the obsolescence of poetry spurred Peacock's friend Percy Bysshe Shelley into writing 'A Defence of Poetry'. When Prynne titled his collection BRASS, it seemed like an endorsement of poetry's inadequacies in the face of vastly more powerful discourses. Prynne does not endow the poet with powers that do not belong to him, but he does urge us to mount a defence *now*. Poetry must be written in good faith with the world. Those who are not made uncomfortable enough by their presence inside the current system to seriously question the privileged moment of lyric utterance may find posterity doubts their faith.

E

HIROSHIMA

BY

ERIK VAN DER WEIJDE

HE WAS THE FIRST ONE IN THE OFFICE IN THE MORNING AND THE LAST ONE TO LEAVE AT NIGHT

BY

GARTH WEISER

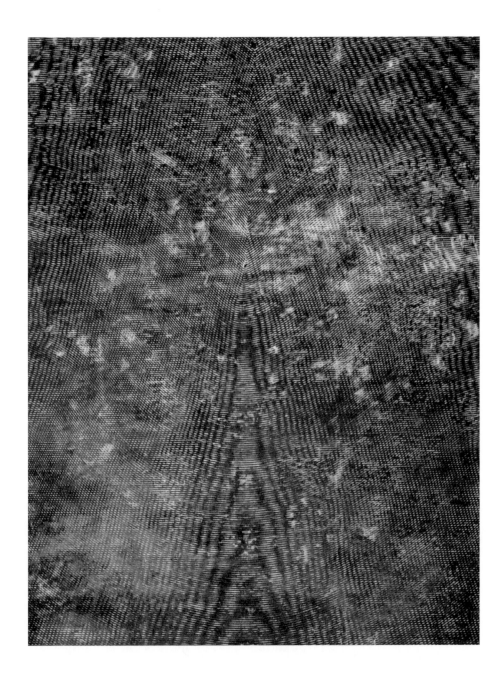

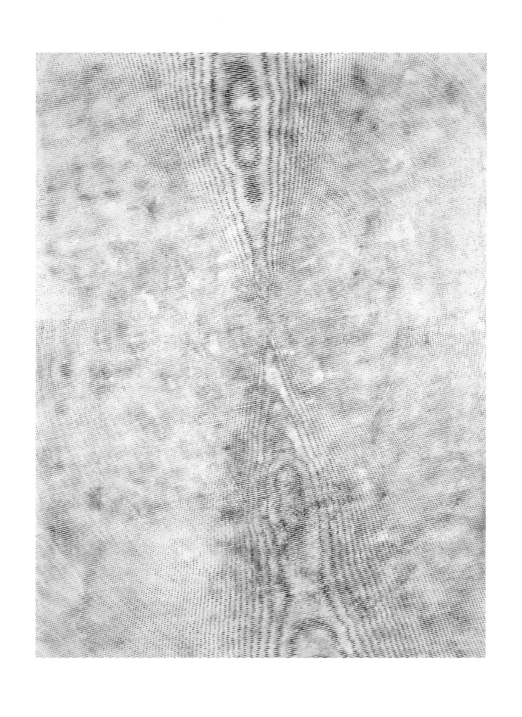

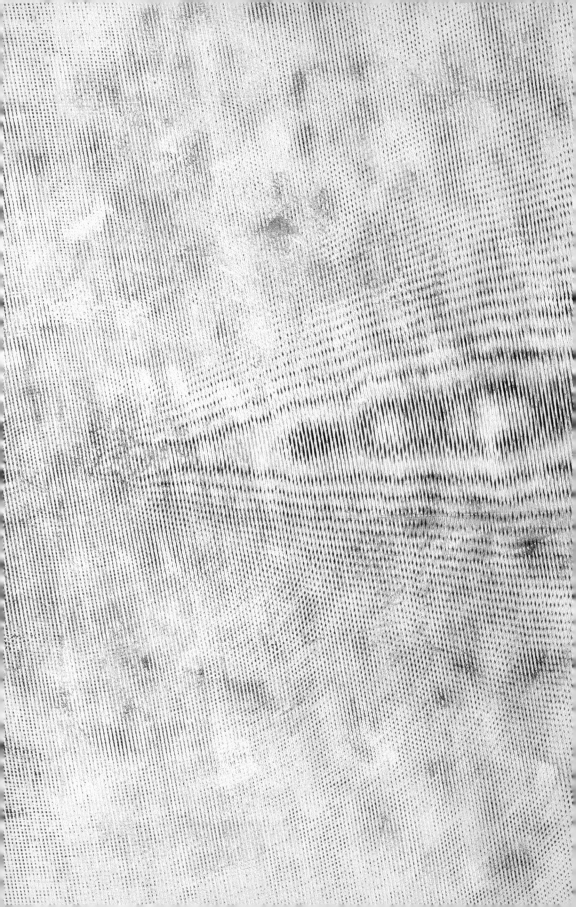

INTERVIEW

WITH

JULIA KRISTEVA

JULIA KRISTEVA IS PRINCIPALLY KNOWN FOR HER ROLE IN THE POST-STRUCTURALIST TURN THROUGH WORK IN THE FIELDS OF SEMIOTICS, CRITICAL THEORY AND PSYCHOANALYSIS. Originally from Bulgaria, she began her academic career engaged with the work of post-formalist theorist Mikhail Bakhtin, leading her to formulate the now ubiquitous (though often misconstrued) concept of intertextuality. Moving to France to continue her studies, she quickly gravitated towards TEL QUEL, an avant-garde literary journal that was at the nexus of structuralist and post-structuralist thought in France c. 1960–1980, and found herself at the heart of a group of prominent intellectuals that included her mentor Roland Barthes, Michel Foucault, Jacques Derrida, and her husband-to-be, renowned writer and critic Philippe Sollers.

Often considered one of the three mothers of feminist post-structural theory alongside Hélène Cixous and Luce Irigaray, Kristeva had an ambivalent relationship to the feminist movements of the time, rejecting essentialist feminism and non-radical, reformist trends, while seeking to move beyond the politics of difference towards one founded upon the singularity of each person. Kristeva's thought was nonetheless assimilated into both French and Anglo-American feminist discourse, especially for her reappraisals of maternity, the constitution of subjectivity and the body within the theoretical frameworks of linguistics and psychoanalysis. Kristeva then began attending lectures given by Jacques Lacan, culminating in her becoming a practicing psycho-analyst and member of the International Psychoanalytic Association in 1979.

The intervening years have seen Kristeva treat an ever-expanding range of subjects, from religion to depression to the experience of time. Her bibliography comprises some forty books of philosophy, criticism, psychoanalysis, and fiction, and her latest publication, LEUR REGARD PERCE NOS OMBRES, is composed of a series of letters between herself and Jean Vanier, the founder of L'Arche (an international federation for the housing and care of the mentally disabled), on the subject of the disabled individual's place in the world.

I have had an unusual relationship with Julia Kristeva and her family over the past four years, during which time I've occupied some liminal space between employee and family member. A mutual friend introduced us at a time when she was looking for someone to spend time with her son David, a young man who has lived with a disability from an early age. In the years since, David and I have developed an unconventional but deeply caring friendship that has led to, among other things, a broader understanding of the 'new humanism' his mother has sought to animate through her books, lectures, political action, and more. One day before David and I went off to run around the city together, Julia and I sat down to tea in her spacious apartment near the Jardin du Luxembourg to talk about her theoretical innovations, her political engagements, and her book with Jean Vanier.

———————————

Q. THE WHITE REVIEW — You have created and rethought a significant number of conceptual terms over your career – intertextuality, abjection, the semiotic, and so on. The spaces that you explore through these concepts were quickly appropriated by academia, particularly in the fields of literature, philosophy and psychoanalysis, leading to a more or less democratic propagation of your ideas. What kind of new conceptual spaces have you been exploring in recent years?

A. JULIA KRISTEVA — It is true that for a certain number of academics, it seems that I suspended my theoretical activities in the eighties. I tend to be associated with the notions I created and developed – intertextuality, abjection, and the semiotic versus the symbolic – but I don't see myself through this prism. When I arrived in France as a semiotician, my conceptual preoccupations were implicitly political, and especially so through the intermediary of ethics. Intertextuality – the idea that a text is built at the intersection of other texts, both anterior and posterior, and asserting that this is the manner in which a text inscribes itself in history and the social pact – opened up structuralism and its formalist derivatives by associating them with subjective experience and social conflict. The notion of abjection [a complex concept concerning the experience of coming into contact with that which is outside the symbolic order and thus horrifies or repulses] led me to the history of religions and their 'purification' programmes, ranging from Levitical taboos and Buddhist rites concerning food to the language in which, according to Christians, purity resides (or doesn't). My thought on this subject also brought me to confront a monument of modern horror: the work of Louis–Ferdinand Céline, whose novels are as fascinating in their rhetorical mastery as his pamphlets are in their abjection.

As for the semiotic and the symbolic (the first pertaining to pre-language and the second to the rule of syntax), these concepts brought me to explore the role of the literary genre-deconstructing avant-garde, and this approach in turn opened the door to the pictorial avant-garde. This is a great pleasure for me, as it means I get to work on the most interesting subjects of a period. This concern that is at once literary, theoretical, and ethical/political, is continued through my interest in foreigners, as well as in the exclusion of other groups. The exclusion of women, which persists despite the various advances of feminism, has of course been of special interest to me, and it has led to my work on female genius. Last but not least, I have always been interested in the vast realm of religion, from which aesthetics is inseparable. I recently delved into this with a work on the need to believe, as well as with a large volume on the experience of that great Catholic saint descended from Marranos, Thérèse of Lisieux.

Q. THE WHITE REVIEW — Are there any contemporary philosophers, authors, or critics that are currently opening new horizons for your thought?

A. JULIA KRISTEVA — Like everyone else, I live in a hyper-connected society, and I try not to overlook publications by X, Y, or Z; but the creation we might hyperbolically call 'the life of the mind' essentially depends on a person's initiative to express him or herself. So, I try more to explore the shadows of my own experience rather than to follow along the paths of others, which, while they are of interest to me, are not guides for my thought.

Q. THE WHITE REVIEW — You have had some influence in politics over the past few years – that is to say, while you have been politically engaged from the beginning and your ideas have had political consequences, your reputation now allows you to be heard when you write an open letter to the French President, as you did on the subject of the handicapped [in French: handicapés] in 2003. Do you find that your thought has become less theoretical and more pragmatic since you've captured the attention of politicians?

^{A.} JULIA KRISTEVA — I have always considered politics to be present from the outset. You could say that the current formulation of my work is less abstract and less technical, but certainly not more political than before. In any case, I don't feel it to be so. For me, politics is far from being the *nec plus ultra* that will save the world; quite to the contrary, it is revealing its limits more and more, as it is subject to the logic of finance and virtual communication. Ethics, however, is a subject that has always been of concern to me, and one from which I consider my work to be inseparable, from the much more technical period of my earlier work to the current, more public period.

^{Q.} THE WHITE REVIEW — How might psychoanalysis attend to and shed light on mental handicaps?

^{A.} JULIA KRISTEVA — Each disability is singular, and I severely condemn the labelling of handicapped people with this or that difficulty, be it neuronal, psychological, or other. I say this because it is of the utmost importance that we refuse to conflate a person with their situation. In France, we say 'a person in a stuation of handicap' instead of a handicapped person, which is not simply a lexical question but a political and ethical one. If you consider that the person in a situation of handicap is a singularity and that he or she has verbal, preverbal, or transverbal codes of communication, then psychoanalysis is able to lend an ear. It is up to psychoanalysis to adapt in order to be attentive to a person's way of expressing themselves, of communicating. I worked with someone who would be considered mildly autistic according to the terminology often employed, and who, at 3 or 4 years old, still wasn't communicating with language. But through the introduction of music, through sung performance, this person's

notions began taking the form of little operas, and I assisted this child in becoming a young man who now speaks and expresses himself reasonably well. Once again, each person undertaking analysis is singular – I don't give an outline for treating or accompanying this or that handicap, but I do advocate the need for psychoanalysis to become more complex, to adapt so that it might be attentive to the singularities of those undertaking analysis.

^{Q.} THE WHITE REVIEW — You hadn't written much on the experience of being the mother of a handicapped child prior to your book with Jean Vanier. How did you come to write more explicitly on the subject?

^{A.} JULIA KRISTEVA — Well, that's not entirely the case. There is always a young boy with some sort of problem in my fiction. My novel *POSSESSION*, for example, is the story of a mother who plans to assassinate her deaf son's speech therapist. But I find it obscene when parents imagine themselves in their children's place – especially when it comes to children in a situation of handicap – and judge or glorify them while expressing what they imagine their children might express. That is my general feeling regarding autobiography, so I create characters to communicate certain thoughts or experiences through transposition. I think that we end up lying when we try to speak truthfully about our lives. That's why psychoanalysis was invented, to help us be more authentic.

^{Q.} THE WHITE REVIEW — In your letters to Jean Vanier, you write about founding a new humanism – that this new humanism would embrace marginalised people by way of what you call 'encounters', perhaps leading to a mind–opening experience or, for Jean Vanier, a spiritual awakening.

XXXIII

A. JULIA KRISTEVA —— I believe that humanism is an important idea, and even though Greek and Jewish thought paved the way for it internally, its origins lie in Christian humanism. This Christian humanism crystallised in the idea of care – of care for human beings – and the dignity specific to each person. In order to understand how this care and dignity specific to all concerns people in situations of handicap, we have to remember that the way we have of thinking of handicap comes to us from the field of medicine in general and, to a degree, the humanities. It goes back to Aristotle, to Greek medicine and thought, which designates the symptom as a lack, a defect, or a poverty. Aristotle employs the term *steresis* for this idea of privation – if you are blind, it must be that you don't 'have' god, that your eyes are deficient, or if you have motor difficulties it's that you are missing legs. And from this idea of privation, Christian humanism forged the idea of the handicapped person, designated as the poor person.

Lack is still a crucial element in the idea of the poor person – the poor person is lacking something – but Christian humanism declared that the poor person deserves compassion, which is to say that we should share his suffering, that we should feel it with him, help and support him. This idea was first expressed in the Gospel of Matthew 25:35 ('For I was hungry, and you gave me food: I was thirsty, and you gave me drink: I was a stranger, and you took me in…'), and developed into the idea of giving what is lacking. The sick, foreigners, prisoners, and the handicapped are all encompassed in this category of the poor, and Christianity went on to develop a strategy to support these people, notably with the advent of charitable orders. The first to put this into practice was a Byzantine monk named Zoticus. It was Zoticus who observed that in Byzantium, in Greece, the handicapped were exhibited in the public square – people having realised that the handicapped were affected by something different from other lacks, something irremediable in view of contemporary knowledge – before the eyes of the gods, supposedly offering them to the gods, which is to say that they went without treatment. Zoticus objected to this and founded what was, in a way, the first charitable order.

What were the advantages of this? As concerns science, the entire field of medicine grew from it. Despite its many problems, I'm not entirely opposed to the medical approach – you learn a great deal about vision in general when you treat people whose sight is impaired, and this knowledge can also be extremely helpful to those with unimpaired vision. So, in taking care of those who are lacking you can also better service those who are whole. All pathologies help us better understand the workings of the human body. This logic, by the way, leads to the development of solidarity. One disadvantage, though, is that there is a risk of shutting the handicapped person – considered as poor, lacking, or deficient – into an attitude that renders him infantile, and thus isolates him socially. Whether we take care of him or not, the idea remains that he does not have a place with others, which reduces him once more to a defect.

The word handicap is very poorly chosen and there is a great push against it, but it is also apt in indicating something irremediable, something faulty or deficient. The French Enlightenment thinkers were the first to directly refuse this isolation of the handicapped. It's important for me to recognise the good things they did, since I generally complain about how France is behind the times. It was Diderot – and Rousseau to a lesser degree, but especially Diderot – who took this stance. His *LETTRE*

Sur les Aveugles à L'usage de Ceux qui Voient (Letter on the Blind) and his *Lettre Sur les Sourds et Muets* (Letter on the Deaf and Dumb) transformed the handicapped person from an object of care into a political subject. He was basically saying in these tracts, 'I no longer see you as someone who lacks this or that. Otherwise put, you are not reducible to your symptom, you are a person with the same rights as anyone. Everyone is born free and with equal opportunity, and this opportunity is a political matter.' Here, the handicapped person is admitted as an equal and as a member of a community; he is not exposed before the eyes of God and so on, and this community bears the responsibility of supplementing what lacks – this lack not being regarded as a defect, and this person possessing the right to the same care and the same good as everyone else.

The elevation from the object of care to a political subject was very important, but I do not believe that this politicisation of the handicapped has sufficiently challenged the insulation of the handicapped person in his symptom. Humanism lacks an idea of dignity proper to each person in his singularity and specificity. We have to turn to the history of philosophy in order to meet this task. Duns Scotus, whom I've spoken about quite a lot recently, conceived of the truth as something that inheres neither in an absolute idea (thus applicable to the Supreme Being or God), nor in matter (a deficient organ, for example, or a perfectly functioning one). Human truth, rather, is the singularity of each creature, and this singularity is to be appreciated, to be accepted as it is, and to be communicated with so as to discover our own proper singularities. For Duns Scotus, this encounter with singularity is the source of happiness. I think that this is the vision we neglect to

value today. Why hasn't humanity – why haven't we attended to this? I think that economic difficulties, general misery, and everything else keep most of us from taking this respectful and rewarding conception of singularity seriously. But we who live in what we call 'advanced democracies' *can* make this happen, both economically and politically. We see this happening more and more – all sorts of other singularities that challenge the consensus and conventions, that break down general normativity and generate interest in the right to singularity. I think that if we have to refound humanism, we mustn't do so based on norms but on respect for singularities.

Q. THE WHITE REVIEW —— The way you write about the defects and failures of the handicapped person in a capitalist world run by ultra-efficient super-consumer *übermenschen* tempts me to draw a parallel between the handicapped and the lumpenproletariat...

A. JULIA KRISTEVA —— I see what you mean, but I don't agree. I think that your intuition comes from a generous but generalising vision that places all exclusions, and particularly the most radical exclusions, in the same category. This generous concern leads us to forget people's singularities, and we especially tend to forget that which is specific to people in situations of handicap. What is specific – and I hold this to be very important – is that the person in a situation of handicap provokes a great deal of indifference and occasionally arrogance, both of which serve to hide anxieties – anxieties that are incommensurable with those provoked by a difference in class or religion or by the lumpenproletariat. Why? Because a person in a situation of handicap confronts us with mortality. This is to say that no-one, be he blind, deaf, or mentally disabled, can survive without a prosthesis or an accompaniment.

Thus, we are exposed to our finitude and the fear of death. And this is something for which modern humanism has no philosophy.

Religion has one − though many of us don't accept it − and it has the courage to face mortality. There are priests and rabbis when you're born and when you die and they have a speech for each occasion; but what they have to say is a promise of eternity or paradise or judgment, which is difficult for a rational and scientific person to accept. And so what does the humanist, the humanist who comes to us from the Enlightenment that broke with tradition, have to say before the finitude of human beings? We don't say anything. We know how to approach death. The modern world has an endless procession of commemorations, and we're beginning to address old age because people realise that it could happen to them one day. But it's not the same thing as being born with a handicap or acquiring one through an accident − that is a mortality inside of life, right in the heart of it.

There is a very interesting discovery in the field of biology that I often cite in my lectures. The biologist Jean Claude Ameisen wrote the book *LA SCULPTURE DU VIVANT* (The Sculpture of the Living) in which he explains how from the moment the male and female gametes unite to make life, the cells begin to die − as soon as there is increase there is also decrease. This process is called apoptosis, it's how matter is removed from the merged gametes like stone is chiselled away to make a sculpture. There are any number of cells that have to die off for you to have the nose you have and the mouth you have. But the fact remains that while biology has identified death's work within us, it is difficult to imagine when you're in good health, when you can be having fun and enjoying life.

All the rules of modern life − capitalism, enjoyment, performance, excellence, etc. − run counter to this concern with observing death's work within us. I think that when we neglect this, we remain hardened to different forms of vulnerability, and especially to that vulnerability proper to people in situations of handicap which speaks to the finitude of human life. And maybe the acknowledgment of this finitude can completely change the social contract, the conception of politics, the market, care of the earth, etc. Ecology is just one dimension. We don't need to make an apocalypse out of this finitude, we live with it and we'll go on living for as long as we can, but it is a fact and once we acknowledge that it's there we can reconsider how we relate to those for whom it is always palpably present.

Q. THE WHITE REVIEW —— You have said that it is difficult to inscribe the experience of 'living vulnerability' into cultural codes, but that this is necessary to the 'encounter'. What are the prospects of the handicapped being accepted with open arms given the difficulty of motivating people to act in the interest of something that does not directly concern them? A. JULIA KRISTEVA —— Frankly, I don't have a great deal of hope. The world today is in an endemic crisis without any clear solution in the short run. There are any number of reasons to be pessimistic. At the same time, I've noticed, for example, that the film *INTOUCHABLES* [a French film released in November 2011 about the friendship that develops between a rich humbug quadriplegic and a young *banlieusard* of Senegalese descent who has just finished a short term in prison. It is the second most successful French film in French box office history] moved many people, and the event Jean Vanier and I did together spoke to people,

too. We hope that events such as these will inspire people to follow our example.

Q. THE WHITE REVIEW —— It seems that conceiving of a new humanism would imply conceiving of a new economy – and that calling for a new economy is like challenging Goliath to battle without a sling to hand. How do you imagine we can get to this new humanism without having its more or less pacific revolution collapse?

A. JULIA KRISTEVA —— Well, it's all a question of norms, be they biological norms or economic norms or norms of the masses. Those who act compassionately, such as the religious community or the families of people in situations of handicap, often experience a rejection of the idea of the norm; they say of the handicapped man, 'Abnormal? No, no, I won't say he's abnormal. He's wonderful, he's good.' From my vantage point, from the ideology of haecceity and Duns Scotus' singularity, this idea of the norm and its rejection appears entirely unacceptable because it plays into an insubstantial utopian romanticism. That said, you do have to take into account that the norm itself evolves in modern society. Certain groups who have been marginal but who take a rebellious and creative stance end up moving the norm and give rise to a new pact with the majority – with minority groups first and then little by little with the majority. We see this with the acceptance of abortion, with the acceptance of homosexuality, with the fact that in France the handicapped are allowed to work and that handicapped children are allowed to go to school with non-handicapped children.

The norm evolves slowly, it depends on certain social groups demanding respect, the right to the optimal development of their singularities – here, I'm thinking especially of people in situations of handicap – and that we allow them to integrate into society with a minimum of creativity so that they might have a social life. From there, society itself adapts to them and the norm shifts. So is it possible? Yes. Slowly but surely, at least in the West, the norm is shifting in this sense.

Q. THE WHITE REVIEW —— This question of moving norms brings me to wonder if the new humanism you're talking about isn't the same as what was beginning to emerge forty years ago in the May '68 movement.

A. JULIA KRISTEVA —— I don't know if it's the same as what was going on with the May '68 movement, but there were elements of it that shared this idea of valuing creativity, freeing passions and desires – which was a starting point for the feminist movement – coming out and proudly asserting different sexual orientations and different genders, and so on. What occurred in '68 came about because of what I'll call a romantic eruption. We didn't take the constraints of the question of the norm or the question of the social contract into any consideration whatsoever. There was a temptation to subscribe to an embellished anarchy, which took the form of extremely militarised groups, killers, and assassins in certain countries such as Italy and Germany. I think this tendency was curbed in France because – and what I'm about to say may be a bit exorbitant, but it seems to me to be the case – the May '68 movement was taken very seriously and with a great deal of thought by excellent philosophers and a strong psychoanalytic movement that attempted to clarify the lived experience of the sexual explosion quickly so that it wouldn't become violent. It's important to keep the movement's liberating energy and to see its limits. People generally say that those involved in May '68 have become bosses or apparatchiks, and this is true of some of them, but there are others who write, practice psychoanalysis, direct NGOs, etc. The fabric of society has been infiltrated by this philosophy, and though it might not be the strongest current, it's not dead.

Q. THE WHITE REVIEW —— What are you working on at the moment?

A. JULIA KRISTEVA —— I'm currently collecting essays that I've published or delivered at conferences since 2005 for a book called PULSIONS DU TEMPS. And for the past few years I've been knocking away at a novel I haven't been able to finish. Its working title is a number that just moves me so much. It has to do with the age of Louis XV and his great love, who was not, by the way, Mme de Pompadour, but an astronomical clock that was programmed to run until the year 9999. It seems extremely interesting to me that at the time when the Kingdom of France was beginning to feel the coming revolution and that things were going to change and the sovereignty of Versailles collapse, that there were learned men who were thinking about the year 10000. I took this as an occasion to think about our relationship to time today, women's time, and cosmic time as conceived by our current astronomers. And the acceleration in science requires us to live differently, too – bringing us back to our finitude, which, curiously, doesn't seem to be of great interest to our politicians and philosophers, though everybody from Voltaire to Émilie du Châtelet was interested in these things in the eighteenth century. In a world suffering under the burdens of economic crises and deadly battles, we've lost a dimension proper to the sciences which might be able to help us reflect on human issues differently, too.

JACOB BROMBERG, SEPTEMBER 2012

THE LITERARY CONFERENCE

BY

CÉSAR AIRA

(*tr.* KATHERINE SILVER)

[EDITOR'S NOTE: What follows is the last section from César Aira's novella *THE LITERARY CONFERENCE*. César, the narrator, is a writer and translator who has fallen on hard times due to the global economic downturn. He is also a self-confessed 'mad scientist', intent on world domination. In the first part of the novella, César visits a beach and intuitively solves the ancient riddle of the Macuto Line. His reward is a pirate's treasure — he becomes a very wealthy man. Even so, César's quest for world domination endures. He attends a literary conference to be near the man whose clone he hopes will lead him to victory: the world-renowned Mexican author Carlos Fuentes. César, using a specially-cloned wasp, obtains a cell from Fuentes's DNA and the cloning process begins. Here we join him, bleary-eyed, on the morning after he has watched a performance of one of his own plays. During the course of a drunken night out with student-fans of his work, César has seduced a young woman named Nelly — but only, it seems, because she knows his past love, Amelina.]

F

AT DAWN, THINGS EMERGED FROM THEIR REALITY, as if in a drop
of water. The most trivial objects, embellished with profound reality, made me quiver
almost painfully. A tuft of grass, a paving stone, a scrap of cloth, everything was soft
and dense. We were in the Plaza Bolívar, as lush and leafy as a real forest. The sky
had turned blue, not a cloud in sight, no stars or airplanes, as if emptied of everything;
the sun should have appeared from behind the mountains, but its rays were not yet
touching even the highest peak to the west. The light intensified and bodies projected
no shadows. The dark and the light floated in layers. The birds didn't sing, the insects
must have been asleep, the trees remained as still as in a painting. And, at my feet, the
real kept being born, like a mineral being born atom by atom.

The strangeness that made everything sparkle came from me. Worlds rose out of
my bottomless perplexity.

'So, am I capable of love?' I asked myself. 'Can I really love truly, like in a soap
opera, like in reality?' The question surpassed the thinkable. Love? Me, love? Me, the
brain man, the aesthete of the intellect? Wouldn't something need to happen to make
it possible, some cosmic sign, an event that would turn the course of events around,
an eclipse of a kind…? Inches away from my shoe, one more atom crystallised in
a blaze of transparency, then another… If I could love, just like that, without the
universe getting turned upside down, the only persistent condition that made reality
real was contiguity: that things were next to things, in rows or on plates… No, it was
impossible, I couldn't believe it. Nevertheless… Plop! Another atom of air, in front
of my face, initiating another spiral of splendid combustion. If all conditions can be
reduced to a single condition, it is this: Adam and Eve were real.

Nelly and I, sitting on a stone bench under the trees, were as pale as a sheet of
paper. My features were as drawn as could be, an old man's face, pale, bloodless, my
hair sticking out. I knew this because I was looking at my reflection in the glass of the
Exoscope[1] we had in front of us. The actors of the University Theatre had brought it
to the disco at the end of the party, to pay me a goodbye homage; we danced around it
like savages enacting a rain dance, watching our reflections in miniature and upside
down. Afterward, drunk as they were, they left it behind, and I made the effort to
carry it to the plaza, thinking that sooner or later they would remember it and come
get it – they needed it for the show's official opening.

I had to admit they had done a good job. The dawn was fully reflected in the
Exoscope, and in that dawn, the two of us, as if after the end of the world. With great
effort I turned my eyes away from the instrument's glass and looked directly at Nelly.
Without knowing why, I asked her a stupid question.

'What are you thinking about?'

[1]   The Exoscope is 'an enormous instrument' which looks 'a lot like Duchamp's Large
      Glass'. It was used as a prop in César's play, which even he deemed 'too Dadaist' upon
      watching it performed.

She remained quiet but alert for a moment, her eyes lost in the void.

'Do you hear that, César? What's going on?'

I could have sworn the silence was absolute, though as a foreigner I was unable to determine what was normal or abnormal within that silence. In any case, it was not the silence that was puzzling Nelly. Awakening from my reverie, I heard shouts of alarm, cars suddenly accelerating, sirens, all in a kind of dull buzz that pulsated around me, still not disturbing the otherworldly peace of the city centre, though approaching.

'The birds have stopped singing,' Nelly whispered, 'even the flies have gone into hiding.'

'Could it be an earthquake?' I ventured.

'Could be,' she said noncommittally.

A car drove past the plaza at full speed. Behind it came a military truck full of armed soldiers, one of whom saw us and shouted something, but they were driving so fast we couldn't understand him.

'Look!' Nelly shouted, pointing up.

I looked up and saw a crowd of people on the roof terrace of a building, all staring off into the distance and shouting. The same thing was happening on the balconies of the other buildings around that plaza. Right in front of us the cathedral bells began to ring. In a flash the streets were thronging with cars filled with entire families... It seemed like collective madness. As far as I was concerned, it might have been normal: I didn't know the customs of that city, and nothing precluded this from being what happened every Sunday at dawn: the locals coming out onto their balconies and terraces to check the weather, and shouting out joyfully that it was a beautiful day for their outings and sporting events; the cathedral bells, for their part, calling people to morning services; families leaving early for their picnics... If I hadn't been with Nelly I could have taken it as the normal Sunday routine. But she was extremely puzzled, and even a bit alarmed.

It was obvious that whatever was happening was happening far away, and far away in this small, enclosed valley meant the surrounding mountains. We couldn't see them from the plaza, but there were panoramic views from any of the adjacent streets, one of the city's great tourist attractions. I stood up. Nelly must have been thinking the same thing because she also got up and quickly figured out the closest spot where we could find out what was happening.

'Let's go to the archway on Humboldt Street,' she said, already starting off. That archway, which I was familiar with, was about one hundred yards away; it stood at the foot of a very long public stairway that was so steep you could see half the valley from there. I started to follow her, then stopped her with my hand.

'Should we leave this monstrosity here?' I asked, pointing to the Exoscope.

She shrugged. We left it and walked off quickly. In the brief time it took us to get to the archway, just a short distance away, the activity in the streets had increased so much it was difficult to make our way through the crowds. Everybody was nervous, some were terrified, most were rushing around as if their lives depended on it. Everyone was talking, but I couldn't understand a word, as if they were speaking foreign languages, which must be a natural effect of panic.

When we got there, we saw it. It was so astonishing it took a while for me to absorb. To begin with, we saw that the alarm was justified, to say the least. I don't know exactly how to describe it. At first, it was otherworldly; it was still dawn, the sun hadn't yet appeared, the sky was very clear and very empty, bodies projected no shadows … and colossal blue worms were slowly descending from the mountain peaks... I'm aware that stating it like this might bring automatic writing to mind, but stating it is my only choice. It seems like the insertion of a different plot line, from an old B-rated science fiction movie, for example. Nevertheless, the seamless continuity had at no time been interrupted. They were living beings, of this I was certain: I had too much experience manipulating life forms to make that mistake. There are some movements no machine can imitate. I calculated the size of the worms: they were approximately one thousand feet long and seventy feet in diameter; they were almost perfect cylinders, with no heads or tails, although their geometric form had to be mentally reconstructed because they were coiling and twisting and changing shape as they moved across the anfractuous mountain terrain. They also looked soft and slimy, but their formidable weight could be deduced by observing them displace enormous rocks along their way, sunder the mountainside, and reduce whole trees to splinters. The most extraordinary thing, which would have been worthy of admiration had the circumstances not added an extra touch of terror, was their colour: a phosphorescent blue with watery tones, like an almost darkened sky, a blue that seemed dampened by fresh placentas.

Nelly grabbed my arm. She was horrified. I swept my eyes along the perimeter of this great Andean amphitheatre: there were hundreds of worms, all descending toward the city. From the shouts, which I quickly began to understand, I learned that the same thing was occurring in the mountains behind us, the ones we couldn't see from where we stood. I've already said that Mérida is completely surrounded by mountains. This meant only one thing: very soon we would be crushed by the monsters. The landslides they were provoking were cataclysmic; the entire valley shook as stones the size of houses tumbled down the slopes, and there was probably already vast destruction on the outskirts. A simple projected calculation revealed that the city was doomed. Two or three of these worms would be enough to leave no brick standing. And there were hundreds of them! Moreover, with horror and despair I realised that the quantity was indefinite … and increasing. It was as if they kept being

F

born, and the process showed no signs of stopping.

The ones in front were already halfway between the highest peaks and the valley floor. That's why they were descending: their own multiplication was forcing them downhill. It was an almost mechanical destiny, not one due to any murderous impulse on the part of these strange beasts. In fact, they were much too strange to harbour any agenda. Their size was what would destroy us… If anyone entertained a hope that their size was an optical illusion, and that they would get smaller as they descended until they appeared as inoffensive as cigarette butts under the soles of our shoes, they would have to dismiss the idea: they were very real, and having one nearby would be a terminal experience.

Any hope regarding the relativity of their size was painfully dispelled a few minutes later, when we witnessed the following episode from where we were standing under the archway. Several military trucks, the one we had seen driving past the plaza and others, converged on a road that rose in the direction of the worms. We saw them stop when they reached the one nearest the city. The soldiers got out and fanned out in front of the blue mass. At that moment denial was no longer possible: the men looked like insects next to the monster – and pathetically ineffectual. This became obvious once they began to shoot at it with their machine guns. They didn't miss their target once (it was like aiming at the mountain itself), but they could have continued for an eternity to the same effect, that is, to no effect. The bullets disappeared into the soft tons of blue flesh like pebbles tossed into the sea. They tried bazookas, cannons, hand grenades, even antiaircraft missiles fired from the hood of one of the trucks, all with the same derisive futility. The climax came when the worm, in the course of its blind march, slid down a steep slope and one section of its body rolled onto the road, crushing trucks and men like an enormous rolling pin, reducing them to laminas. The survivors ran off in terror. The crowd broke their awed silence as they watched the events unfold, and I heard cries and shouts of anguish. Their worst fears were being confirmed. Somebody pointed to another spot, to one side, where another catastrophe was taking place: it was the highway that led across the plateau and out of the valley. Another worm had fallen over a compact line of cars trying to escape, causing innumerable fatalities. Traffic came to a standstill, and people abandoned their cars and ran between the rocks and bushes back toward the city. There was no escape. This was definitive. Eyes turned with fear toward the old colonial buildings around us: the city itself seemed to be the last possible refuge, and it was an illusion to think that its feeble walls could withstand the weight of the worms.

The collective attention turned back to itself, as if to confirm the reality of what was occurring through the reaction of fear. And I was implicated in this reversion. Like so many others, like everybody, perhaps, I have always thought that in a real collective catastrophe I would find the material of my dreams, take it in hand, shape it,

F

finally; then, even if only for an instant, everything would be permitted. It would take something as grand and widespread as an earthquake, an interplanetary collision, or a war to make the circumstances genuinely objective and thus make room for my subjectivity to take hold of the reins of action.

But the subjective was made manifest even in the supremely objective. The examples of cataclysms hereby offered, which in reality are not examples, do not include the invasion of enormous slimy creatures. That would never happen in real life; it rises out of a feverish imagination, in this case mine, and returns to it as a metaphor for my private life.

Here I have again reached the moment to change levels, to make another 'translation'. But this one is so radical that it comes full circle and reties the plot line exactly where I left it.

The mental process of the character representing me in the previous 'translation', from the point at which he was contemplating the benefits of a collective catastrophe, apparently dissolved entirely into fiction, then gathered up all the loose ends and elaborated a generalised reinterpretation, not only of the previous 'translations' but of the process itself out of which 'translations' arise.

Just as when interpreting a nightmare, I was assailed by a sudden doubt: might it be my fault? A priori, this seemed absurd, an extreme manifestation – exaggerated to the point of caricature – of the lack of proportion between small causes and grand effects. But one thing led to the next, and in a vertiginous process this conjecture became more and more plausible. I went back and reviewed my own 'translations' until I found the root of them all, the device from which they had emerged. In my mind, the march of the worms became retrograde, and with the same brutal blindness with which they were descending, they turned and climbed back up, destroying my inventions, from whose crushed cadavers rose little clouds of memory, ghosts of memory.

Because I had forgotten everything. The same system that created my thoughts took charge of erasing them, turning them into sinuous white strips that reached across every level. How can there be so much amnesia in a single lifetime? Isn't this a point in favour of the theory of reincarnation?

Of course, there is such a thing as 'blind translation', the act of mechanically transposing one language to another, without passing through the content, which is what professional translators do when they come across a technical and detailed description of a machine or a process… In order to understand what it's about, they would need to consult a manual on the subject, study something they know nothing about and doesn't interest them… But that isn't necessary! By translating correctly, sentence by sentence, the entire page, the translation will turn out well, they will continue to be as happily ignorant as they were at the beginning, and they will get

F

paid for their work. After all, they are paid to know the language, not the subject matter.

The inverted vortex of the titanic herd of blue worms was located somewhere in the mountains. They emerged from that spot into the light and began to slither – even before they came fully into view – along the broken horizon of the peaks, like a ball circling the top of the roulette wheel, until they stopped, made their appearance, and began to descend. There were so many and their issuance was so constant that they were all descending at once from all points around the circle (in that particular game of roulette, all the numbers came up at once). I could pinpoint the locus of their emergence, and I was the only person who could: it was the cloning machine. It couldn't be anything else. The years I had devoted full time to the manipulation of cloned materials had so refined my sixth sense that I could recognise it. These worms had all the characteristics; their very excess – where would that come from if not the uncontrolled multiplication of cells that only the cloning machine could generate? Functional beings have inviolable limits. My first thought was that the machine was malfunctioning, had gone haywire. But I immediately corrected myself; that thought was worthy only of a citizen of a consumer society who buys a microwave or a video camera and is overwhelmed by its complexity. This was not the case with me, because I had invented the cloning machine, and nobody knew better than I that it was infallibly rational.

As I have already mentioned, the worms' colour and texture were their most noticeable characteristics. They are also what led me to the heart of the matter. Because that colour, that very peculiar brilliant blue, immediately reminded me of the colour of Carlos Fuentes's cell, which my wasp had brought me... Though when I saw that colour in the cell it did not evoke what it was evoking now that I was seeing it extended over vast undulating surfaces. I now realised I had seen that same colour somewhere else, the very same day the cell had been taken, one week before. Where? On the tie Carlos Fuentes was wearing that day! A splendid Italian raw silk tie, over an immaculate white shirt ... and a light grey suit ... (one memory led to another until the picture was complete). And this horrendous piece of evidence revealed the magnitude of the error. The wasp had brought me a cell from Carlos Fuentes's *tie*, not his body. A groan escaped my lips.

'Stupid wasp and the accursed mother who made you!'

'What?' Nelly asked, surprised.

'Don't pay any attention to me, I understand myself.'

The fact is, I couldn't blame her. It was all my fault. How could that poor disposable cloned tool know where the man stopped and his clothing began? For her it was all one, it was all 'Carlos Fuentes'. After all, it was no different than what happened when the critics and professors who were attending the conference found it

F

difficult to say where the man ended and his books began; for them, too, all of it was 'Carlos Fuentes'.

I saw it with the clarity of the noonday sun: the silk cell contained the DNA of the worm that had produced it, and the cloning machine, functioning perfectly, had done nothing more than decode and recode the information, with the results we were now witnessing. The blue monsters were nothing more nor less than silkworm clones, and if they had been magnified to that absurd size it was simply because I had set the cloning machine to run in 'genius' mode. Under other circumstances I would have smiled with melancholic irony upon seeing to what awkward and destructive gigantism literary greatness could be reduced when it was passed through the weave and warp of life.

I came to my senses after having lost myself in thoughts that rushed through me like a hiccup, and I felt an urgency to do something, anything, to prevent the imminent catastrophe. Regrettably, I have no talent for improvisation. But this was the time for action, not regrets. I would think of something. And even if I didn't, everything would turn out well. If I had started it, I could end it. If it had come out of me, it had to return to me. It couldn't be that I would be responsible for the deaths of several tens of thousands of innocent people and the utter devastation – no stone would remain standing – of this old city. The very possibility of the disaster cast over my being a demonic splendour. In my role as a writer, I am inoffensive. What more could I want than to be diabolical, a destroyer of worlds?! But it is impossible. Well reasoned, however, therein lie the benefits of the changes in level, because then I could, in reality, be a diabolical being, an evil monster: such things are fairly relative, as everyone knows from daily experience.

I grabbed Nelly by the shoulder, and we left the group under the archway. The entire crowd was dispersing, women and men moving suddenly and without any apparent purpose. What could they do? Hide in a cellar? Make final arrangements? In the end, they had to do something.

Nelly was in shock. I brought my face up to hers and spoke to provoke a response from her.

'I'm going to do something. I think I can stop them.' She looked at me incredulously. I repeated, 'If anyone can save the city, I can.'

'But, how?' she stammered, looking behind her.

'You're going to have to help me,' which wasn't altogether true, among other reasons because I still hadn't devised a plan. But it worked, her eyes recovered a glimmer of interest. She must have remembered that I was the hero of the Macuto Line and that performing feats of historical proportion was not unknown to me.

We didn't have to go far. We literally bumped into an empty car that had its motor running and the door open; its owner must have joined the group watching events

F

from the archway.

'Let's go!' I said. I got in behind the wheel. Nelly sat in the passenger seat. We drove off. It was a taxi, an old Pontiac from the seventies, as long and wide as only cars in Venezuela can be today.

I feared the streets would be blocked, but they weren't. The paralysis of uncertainty persisted throughout the city. I sped up, and we came to Viaduct Avenue. The only solution I could think of was to find a way through the newborn beasts, reach the cloning machine, and turn it off. In this way at least I could stop their emergence. I didn't know if putting the machine in reverse would reabsorb the worms, but I could try. In the meantime, I stepped on the gas. We were soon on the viaduct, where we commanded an excellent view of the blue masses slithering down the mountains.

'Where are we going?' Nelly asked. 'I don't think we can escape.'

'That is not my intention, quite the contrary. I'm going to try to get to the place where they are coming from,' at which point I inserted a tiny white lie, because I didn't want her to guess that I was responsible for the disaster. 'What we have to do is close the … hole they are coming out of, and perhaps make them go back … underground.'

She believed me. It was absurd, but in a certain way it evoked the spring mechanism of the Macuto Line, over which I had already been triumphant, and this lent it a patina of truth.

I kept climbing, driving faster and faster. The old Pontiac vibrated, its panels rattling. Driving helped me recuperate some of my lost coordination; a sleepless night and the alcohol had left every cell in my body dead tired. I was overwhelmed with exhaustion. But the internal adrenalin bath sustained my movements, and slowly I recovered my faculties.

I turned left onto a small, very steep street, shifted into first gear, and floored the gas until the motor roared. In a final effort the clunker carried us onto the highway that circled the city. I turned right, moving in the same direction as the morning breeze; snakes and rats, escaping in terror from the mountains, were scrambling across the asphalt. We could now see from close up what was happening. The blue of the worms filled the windshield. They were everywhere, nearby and far away, and their forward march was inexorable. The route we were taking would be quite dangerous in a matter of minutes, and if not, would become so later on. We heard a few rocks, luckily quite small, falling on the roof of the car. I began to doubt the feasibility of my plan. Reaching the cloning machine seemed like mission impossible. We would have to abandon the car sooner or later, perhaps quite soon; I hoped to drive at least as far as the intersection with the road that continued along the plateau; but I remembered that I had climbed on foot for an hour or more before setting down the machine. And based on the way events were unfolding, this interval would give the worms plenty of time to turn the city into a tabula rasa. That is, if we managed to avoid them and reach our goal. We passed by one that was slithering down the hill about two hundred yards from the road. Seen from close up, they were overwhelming. Their shape, which from far away had seemed so well defined, so worm–like, here turned into a blue mess, cloudlike. Nelly devoured it all with her eyes, in silence. She turned to look back at the city, as if calculating the time left before the inevitable occurred. At that moment I sensed she was remembering something, and, in fact, she let out a choked exclamation and looked at me.

'César!'

'What?' I said, lifting my foot off the gas pedal.

'I forgot about Amelina!'

This surprise completely confused me. At that moment more than ever before, Amelina felt like a myth, the legend of love. I had already resigned myself to never seeing her again, so her name came to me from a distance that was purely linguistic. But Nelly's words carried with them an urgency of reality that forced me to adopt a more practical perspective, as if Amelina really did exist. And, undoubtedly, she did. She was somewhere in the city we saw spread out to our right, small and threatened like the model of a city in the hands of an angry child. The image of Florencia, my childhood love, flitted through my mind, the young and enamoured Florencia, whom I felt had been reborn in Amelina thirty years later. Like in a trick diorama, what was far away looked close and vice versa. Love's ghostly stand–ins, which had shaped my life, were spinning around me, forming a tunnel of black light that I was sinking into.

'Where is she?'

'At her house. She sleeps late and very heavily. We must go wake her up and tell her what's going on!'

What good would that do her? None, of course. And us, even less. But the idea attracted me for two reasons: first, I could see Amelina again, and under savage and peremptory circumstances; second, it was the perfect excuse to abandon my impractical plan of reaching the cloning machine. The very instant I made the decision to go, I became possessed by an almost infantile euphoria, because Nelly's words implied that Amelina still lived alone, she had not gotten married, and she, Nelly, continued to think of her in relation to me, and if she had decided to mention her only under this extremity, it was because our love story was real, it carried across all the translations, it would keep its appointment…

'Let's go,' I said. 'But you'll have to guide me.'

She pointed to the first exit, and I veered off the highway, making the tires screech. We turned our backs on the mountain and the worms, as if to say, 'Who cares!' and we returned to the city along a road I didn't know. She told me that Amelina was still living in one of the student apartments in the Nancy Building, the same one where I

F

had visited her years before. It wasn't far away, but nothing was in such a small city.

The traffic got heavier, though it was still moving because nobody was paying any attention to the traffic lights. I wondered where they were all going. From the terraces, people kept looking toward the mountains with the same expectations, the same alarm, the same dismay. They were not taking any measures, but what could they do? The cars were driving like crazy, all in the same direction...

'Where are they going?' Nelly asked.

Suddenly, I knew: to the airport. It seemed strange that I hadn't thought of that sooner; apparently others had. The only way out was by air. But, even assuming there were still some private airplanes available and that military planes were on their way, many could not be saved, let alone all. The commercial flight arrived at ten and departed at eleven, if they hadn't cancelled it. And if it arrived full of passengers, the passengers themselves would want to remain on the flight back to Caracas.

A Mercedes Benz, its horn blasting like a siren, passed us; I glimpsed Carlos Fuentes and his wife in the back seat, their profiles set in serious expressions. They, too, were on their way to the airport. How naïve! Or, perhaps, they had been offered seats on an official plane? The city was the provincial capital, and surely the governor would have one ... but I found it hard to believe that in this predicament of 'save yourself if you can', literary hierarchies would be respected. No way! Surely they were going to try to somehow wangle a seat, like so many others... I remembered that I had a reservation for the eleven o'clock flight, I was even carrying the ticket in my pocket... If I had been able to catch up with that powerful Mercedes I would have offered them my seat... I've always liked Carlos Fuentes; not in vain had I chosen him for my experiment. I felt like a scoundrel. Everything that was happening was my fault, and now, instead of putting everything on the line to rid the world of this threat (it was the least I could do), I was allowing myself to be carried away by a private, sentimental whim; I was ashamed of my lack of responsibility.

To appease my conscience, I said out loud, 'It will take us only a few minutes. Then all three of us will go to the mountain.'

She indicated where to turn and continued directing me along a sinuous route. She leaned forward and pointed her finger in the direction I should go. I couldn't avoid looking at her, and I seemed to be seeing her, again, for the first time. Again I discovered her beauty, her youth ... a bit excessive for me, but that's what it was all about. To be young again, 'good and beautiful', as she had said. She was mysterious, that little Nelly, her serenity and silence shielded some kind of secret that enthralled me...

Here there is a blank in the story. I don't know what happened in the following few minutes. Perhaps we never reached Amelina's place, perhaps we got there and didn't find her, or couldn't rouse her. What I do know is that I suddenly found myself about a hundred feet below street level on the banks of a stream through a deep gorge that crosses the valley and the city longitudinally. Behind me, far above, was the viaduct, the most centrally located bridge connecting the two sides of the gorge. A large crowd had gathered on the other side and was watching me. In front of me, almost perfectly still, was a worm. He was little more than fifty feet away. Apparently the monster had rolled there: his descent had been brutal, judging from what he had left in his wake: fallen trees, houses smashed to smithereens. His congeners must have been surrounding the city in a deadly grip. I looked around. The balconies of the buildings along the edge of the gorge were full of people, eager to witness the confrontation. I recognised the Nancy Building, whose pinkish walls emitted an opaque hue that tinged everybody with their colour.

But I had to hurry. The sense of urgency was the only thing that had survived my amnesia. My hands were clutching the vertical bars of the Exoscope, and Nelly was holding the other end. I saw her through the glass panels. How had we gotten there, and with that device? I didn't have time to reconstruct it all, but I could imagine it. Upon seeing the worm fall into the deep riverbed, the lowest level it could reach, I must have thought it would be at my mercy, at least for a few minutes, so I could test an annihilation experiment. We probably ran to the plaza, several hundred feet away, to get the Exoscope, then carried it (this was evident from how every muscle in my body ached) and lowered it from the viaduct: the rope still attached to it was testimony enough.

Whatever the nature of the experiment, I didn't even have to think about it because my brain, in parallel, was already making the calculations...

'A little more ... here ... slowly ...'

Poor Nelly was panting from the effort. We stood the Exoscope up in front of the worm and carefully turned the glass panels. A fraction of an inch in either direction would make all the difference. I saw the worm's reflection and touched its image in the cold glass with the tips of my fingers. Though threatening, brutal, as lethal as a soft skyscraper come to life, it was beautiful, a masterpiece. I am fascinated by what is huge, excessive. Perhaps never before had such a creature trodden upon the earth, a being made of blue silk, so artificial and at the same time so natural. All its fascination resided in its magnification. It was still a miniature, on which the limitless freedom of size had operated.

I turned to look at it directly. It had moved closer. Though it had no face, it had a vague expressiveness that seemed to speak of its horror at having been born, its feeling of not being welcome, of having landed where it wasn't wanted. I could have stayed there for hours contemplating it. After all, I had good reason to believe it to be my masterpiece. I would never again create anything like it, even if I wanted to. What gave it that particular blue hue was the depth of its materiality, the fact that each cell

F

was composed of reality and unreality. As if my gaze were stimulating it, it began to move, though most likely it had never stopped moving. It covered the distance between us with what was probably, for it, no more than a shudder. Nelly took refuge behind me; the audience held its breath. I lifted my eyes to its formidable mass – the height of a five-storey building. It was now or never.

Just as it was supposed to happen, at that instant a ray of sun shone through a break in the mountains and in a straight line onto the glass of the Exoscope. I expertly moved the panels so that the yellow point would draw a tiny square. I knew well the effect this action of the light would have on the cloned cells. And, indeed, the worm began to get reabsorbed into its own reflection in the glass. It was very quick, very fluid, but it was not without incident. The structure of the Exoscope shook, and I was afraid it would fall over. I held one end with all my strength and asked Nelly to do the same on the other. She obeyed me, in spite of her fear. It seemed as if it were going to break apart, but we held firm, and the worm kept going and going … When less than a tenth of its mass was still materialised, it coiled up around us. I closed my eyes. I felt it slipping, almost brushing up against me, and the blue colour penetrated me even through my lowered eyelids. When I lifted those lids, it had finished its re-entry… Or, rather, it hadn't. One last fragment of blue substance remained, which, perhaps because it was the last, rose up in a violent whirlwind on Nelly's end then quickly got sucked into the glass. The movement made one of her shoes fly off, and I saw that her foot was wounded.

The Exoscope was still. I leaned over to look into the glass. There it was, a transparent blue phylactery dissolving into atoms and mixing up with the golden atoms of the sun in a furious battle, in an inoffensive, artistic game that dispersed in seconds. But one drop of blood on Nelly's foot had splashed onto the glass. In a swish, the atomic beam carried it away into the depth of the transparency.

I stood back. It was over. The audience applauded and cheered, joyous honking began to resound throughout the city. The entire herd of gigantic worms had disappeared, dissolved into the dawn air. People took it as some kind of miracle, but I, of course, knew that clones were like that: one is all.

I examined my friend's foot, which was bleeding profusely. Men and boys were climbing down the gorge, and the first to arrive offered to carry her up; the wound wasn't serious, but she needed to be taken to the emergency room to be bandaged. I climbed up behind them, and when they'd gotten her into the car, I told her that I was leaving on the morning flight, as planned. She promised to come to the airport to say goodbye.

F

The Literary Conference was originally published by New Directions in the US and is forthcoming from Hamish Hamilton in the UK.

F

FRAGMENTS FROM ARCHILOCHUS IN THE NORTH

BY

SARAH HESKETH

ARCHILOCHUS IN THE NORTH

I

I am a man of common talents:
a teller of tales, a filler,
a fettler, a drinker,
a fear–nothing maker.

2

The mill's the mother of all invention.
The mill's a mother that eats her own young.
Look, here's a valley of blackened teats.

3

There are green hills that shoulder this land.
The wind a fine cloth over the stones.

4

A fixed people,

        picking at fleeces.

5

      He starts his tale a long way from the end.

6

Fat cobbles, knuckles in a punch,
each street is bent with the effort
of holding us all up. All towns
look small under the rain;
the clock towers telling us
that we are always late; shadows
black stains across the brickwork.
Nobody hopes for anything but the same:

                King Cotton.

7
[*A rag of paper,*
but]

Scraped sky.
We are all

Unnumbered
Smoky tops

Hands
clatter-song of the looms.

                                                        8
                                                 Mizzling.

                                           9
                                    Here's a man
                                    who knows just what it's like
                                    starting the day
                                    with both feet in one clog.

10
Poverty [　　　] *my loom* [
　　　　　　　] *Gaffer's too skinny to pay*
Poverty [　　　　　　] *on the clock*
[　　　　　] *me shuttle*
　Poverty [　　　　]

11
Carded wool.

12
My poor blind ears.

13
Clackety, clackety, clackety, clackety.

P

14
Spindle
[   ]
[   ]
        and mule.

15
She knows just how
to kiss that shuttle.

16
Expect with one hand
and spit in the other
and see which gets full first.

17

The same dumb lover for us all:
days lost in the valleys of her wooden applause.
Kisses spun fast from a dirty wet thread.

Children cry out between her legs.
Their deft fingers picking at a greasy weft.
Silk will be the ruin of us all.

Lady Jenny, leading, then leaving us.
That which gets thrown across.

THE LITERARY OUROBOROS
(OR TWENTY-ONE PARAGRAPHS ON THE INCOMPLETE IN LITERATURE)

BY

SCOTT ESPOSITO

'THROUGHOUT HIS LIFE, Richardson constantly patrolled his works in the interests of "polite letters", erasing solecisms, "low" terms, mistakes of social manners and potential indelicacies, anxiously approximating his occasionally horny-handed prose to the standards of gentility. ... But his most vital revisions were not simply questions of etiquette. The chief purpose of this exhausting labour was to control the interpretations of his texts. Exasperated by perverse critics who found Lovelace attractive and Clarissa over-scrupulous, Richardson added to the novel a plethora of material designed to insulate it against such misprisions. The irony of this enterprise has already been suggested: the more Richardson plugs and patches to disambiguate his writing and avert incorrect readings, the more he piles on matter for yet further misconstruction. Driven on by what must surely be seen as a quasi-pathological urge for perfection, Richardson succeeds in unravelling his text a little more, prising it open in the act of trying to spring it shut. In striving to "complete" his work, to achieve the utterly definitive text, he simply sets himself more to do.' Terry Eagleton, THE RAPE OF CLARISSA (1982)

Terry Eagleton, who argues for the importance of CLARISSA to the postmodern era, proceeds to say, with only partial irony, that Samuel Richardson was only stopped from revising the book by death. These continual augmentations may not have been the best idea: it must be noted that, because of its length (it is one of the longest works ever written in English), CLARISSA is rarely read outside of English departments, and, probably, rarely read inside of them as well. Its initial incarnation saw the light of day in 1748: it is a mammoth epistolary novel about the titular woman, who is seduced by the caddish Lovelace. Following Eagleton's reasoning, if Richardson hadn't died he might now still be revising it, and, presuming an immortal Richardson, the book could very well be theoretically infinite. I do not picture this infinity as an extension of Clarissa's and Lovelace's lives into old age; rather, I picture it as a gradual slowing of time, a monumental expansion of each moment in their romance as the words between them proliferate. Eagleton tells us that Clarissa and Lovelace write each other tens of thousands of words each day, far more than any person would be capable of. If Richardson kept writing, it would grow to twenty thousand, thirty; their romance would not lengthen so much as become dissected into finer and finer bits. This might allow Richardson the perfection of message he so dearly wanted, but if CLARISSA really did grow to be infinite, who would be able to read it? Who could absorb its perfectly controlled message? Better yet, who would want to? That would require a lifetime of reading just one book, in effect a reading life in thrall to an author who would not trust you to gauge his message for yourself.

'I am this month one whole year older than I was this time twelve-month; and having

got, as you perceive, almost into the middle of my fourth volume – and no farther than to my first day's life – 'tis demonstrative that I have three hundred and sixty-four days more life to write just now, than when I first set out; so that instead of advancing, as a common writer, in my work with what I have been doing at it – on the contrary, I am just thrown so many volumes back – was every day of my life to be as busy a day as this – And why not? – and the transactions and opinions of it to take up as much description – And for what reason should they be cut short? as at this rate I should just live 364 times faster than I should write – It must follow, an' please your worships, that the more I write, the more I shall have to write – and consequently, the more your worships read, the more your worships will have to read. … write as I will, and rush as I may into the middle of things, as Horace advises, – I shall never overtake myself –'
Laurence Sterne, TRISTRAM SHANDY (1759)

Eagleton claims that CLARISSA was written with a clear didactic purpose: Richardson took great pains to revise any ambiguity out of his text so that only his interpretation of the novel would remain. Sterne, who fought just to keep pace with the speed of his protagonist's life, comes much closer to our modern view of authorship: fighting, Zeno-like, to reach a reality that is forever fleeting. Since Roland Barthes proclaimed the death of the author, we view authors as individuals with only partial, if any, control over what the text says, much less what it means. This is why Eagleton says we consider it 'vulgar' if literature attempts to impart wisdom. We have relinquished the certainties of universal truths for the sands of mimesis; now, our pole-star is depicting reality *as you see it*. Lacking any possibility of success, art becomes the means by which we reveal how we fail to communicate. It discloses the irreconcilable ambiguities that we believe reside within the creative process, and these ambiguities become metaphors for life's other ambiguities. In a world of art for art's sake we chase an impossible truth.

'He goes back to the newspaper and reads that Claudio Magris believes Ulysses's circular journey as he returns triumphantly home – Joyce's traditional, classic, Oedipal, conservative journey – was replaced halfway through the twentieth century by a rectilinear journey: a sort of pilgrimage, a journey always moving forward, towards an impossible point in infinity, like a straight line advancing hesitantly into nothingness.' Enrique Vila-Matas, DUBLINESQUE (2010)

I run. The music I listen to as I perform my circuit is rap. Rap music, for the most part, consists of very small stories, sometimes tens of them in a single song. Rappers are charismatic braggarts who tell tautological tales about their own success: they are successful because they are the kind of people to be successful. (Like many

E

tautologies, this one actually has much more use in the real world than it would seem on paper.) Their logic – hermetic, perfect in its hermeticism, infinitely repeating – resembles the tiny, tight cycles of the beats they expound it over, which are called *loops*. The longest of these loops might repeat at intervals of perhaps ten seconds, and within those loops nest several shorter loops, repeating at smaller intervals. When the music is good, they all sync up with precise proportion and distribution, like a Calder mobile made from ellipsoids. The quality that makes a rap song good to run to is its *sickness*. A sick song is triumphant, transgressive, intimately familiar, vulnerable, and new all at once. For about a month these songs have the power to induce a feeling of euphoria, each day a little less so, until they finally are only capable of giving me a mild feeling of wellbeing. These songs communicate as does a breakdance: they are a virtuoso display of verbal excess, not meant to tell me anything in particular so much as simply compel my admiration at their rich spectacle. Combined with the exertion of running, they make my brain pore with endorphins. Frequently, when I get to the end of my circuit I do not want to stop, so strong is the music within me that it has built up a surplus of aggressive energy that has nowhere left to go, so I release it by pounding my fist into the thick wood of my front door.

Enrique Vila-Matas' book *BARTLEBY & CO.* is about what he terms 'the literature of the No'. It is meant to be a meditation on literary Bartlebys, geniuses who chose to stop writing. They are so-named after Melville's famous 'scrivener', from the story 'Bartleby, the Scrivener: A Story of Wall Street'. Bartleby is the kind of person we might now recognise as a low-level office drone, and one day he, as Melville puts it, 'obstinately refuses to go on doing the sort of writing demanded of him'. Vila-Matas transfers this concept onto great writers, who preferred to give an obstinate 'no' to their creative voices rather than continue following their demands. J. D. Salinger, for instance, Robert Walser, Rimbaud, Melville himself. Vila-Matas claims that Bartlebys are 'beings inhabited by a profound denial of the world'. Rather than exist within the common reality that we all more or less try to participate in, they abscond to a sealed, perfected reality of their own creation. By writing about these writers, he intends to walk 'the only path still open to genuine literary creation; a tendency that asks the question "What is writing and where is it?" and that prowls around the impossibility of the same.' Vila-Matas is following his great modernist forebears in arguing that literature is in failure. In other words, Vila-Matas is following in the footsteps of the literary theorist Jacques Derrida by foregrounding the search, in place of the answer. By failing to discover why the Bartlebys failed to continue writing, Vila-Matas will create a document – in this case the book *BARTLEBY & CO.* – that he considers to be literature. This book is the compression of two realities into a point of perfect density: the one in which he lives, and the one to which the Bartlebys absconded. I imagine the book as a bird's nest of infinitely lengthened strings connecting these two visions of failure.

'If modernism in literature may be defined as a realism of the unrepresentable, then the WAKE turns out to be a proof of realism's impossibility, of the insufficiency of the instruments of mimesis to capture, convey, or even accurately suggest the measureless surreality of dreams.' Michael Chabon, 'What to Make of FINNEGANS WAKE?', THE NEW YORK REVIEW OF BOOKS, 12 July 2012

I have grown tired of statements like Chabon's. Modernism may very well be a 'realism of the unrepresentable', but facile remarks about FINNEGANS WAKE being 'proof of realism's impossibility' only seek to domesticate failure. If modernism really is the realism of the unrepresentable, then it is because the modernists understand failure as a radical gesture, a break with life, with society, with the civilised world. They have no interest in pat statements about 'the measureless surreality of dreams'. Their goal is not mimesis, that is their starting point. Their goal is the impossible, the infinite. Vila–Matas attempts a genuine response to the impossibility of the modernists' task: the bitter weight, and unimaginable intrigue, of writing toward what cannot be written; by contrast, Chabon wants to close Joyce's mountain within a white picket fence. I do not know if Joyce meant FINNEGANS WAKE to represent our dreams. I do not care, and nor do I care if it succeeds or fails at that ambition. What interests me much more is the book's capacity to instil in Chabon a lifelong source of wonder such that it has inspired him to read it on and off for years and to write.

Vila–Matas attributes to Ludwig Wittgenstein the argument that if concepts like good and evil could ever be defined in a single book, 'this book would cause all the other books to explode'. In essence: that one book would assert such awful authority that it would destroy the need for any other thoughts on concepts like good and evil. This certitude would in turn suck the very oxygen from literature, which is driven by a desire for just this kind of knowledge. The impossibility of ever defining these concepts, the very failure of language and morality to encompass them, is in effect what makes literature possible. This is similar to what happens in Borges' story 'The Library of Babel'. His library, which contains everything that could ever be written, is actually a dystopia that makes the creation of literature pointless. When every last word has already been put down on paper, what is the point of trying to write something? You will only be plagiarising someone who has already said it as well as you, and imitating many who have said it better. Still, if Borges' Library of Babel did exist, it is doubtful that it would contain Wittgenstein's theoretical book defining good and evil. As Wittgenstein himself argued, there are some things that are beyond the capabilities of language. Perhaps, however, if such a book could not be written the library itself would take its place. The infinite library might not resolve the question of good and evil, but it would still suffocate creativity under the weight of *everything*. In that case, creativity would have to become something else, not writing but selecting. Those who might guide others through the Library's infinite holdings would exercise a force akin to what we have traditionally viewed as authorial creation.

And perhaps it is possible that, for all intents and purposes, we already live within Borges' Library. In 1876 George Eliot wrote, 'One couldn't carry on life comfortably without a little blindness to the fact that everything has been said better than we can put it ourselves.' I view Borges' story as an abandonment of this blindness, a recognition, once and for all, that the terms of creativity had to shift in the modern era. In contrast to the Borgesians, Eliot was a writer of impossibility in the sense of Richardson and Sterne: 'Everything I have liked best has been a scrape either for myself or somebody else,' she has one character say. 'My painting is the last scrape; and I shall be all my life getting out of it.' Her worlds are circumscribed by the perfection of ideas received from the dawnings of Western civilisation; in adherence to these ideas, her characters scrape against the sheer walls that stand between thought and action. She dramatises the impossible, infinite struggle to live within ideas that have long since been expressed, not the struggle to articulate these ideas. For Eliot, originality inhered in how you sought to accommodate yourself to good and evil, not in how you claimed to explain what good and evil were.

By the time Borges arrived, no longer was our naïveté such that only intellects of Eliot's rank might contend with the truth uttered long ago in *ECCLESIASTES*: 'There is nothing new under the sun.' By contrast, Borges patterned his career on the idea that there was nothing new under the sun, making it a commonplace. The impossibility of creativity was becoming an integral part of literature that all serious writers had to wrestle with. As mathematicians had already done long before them, they learned new and exotic ways to deal with infinity, to hold it and think about it and manipulate it for their purposes.

Richardson attempted to achieve a kind of perfection: the text over which he, as author, would have complete authority. This would have been commensurate with the times in which he wrote, where the scientists of the day dreamed of knowing the universe in full and where political theorists aspired to perfected government. But with the advent of modernism we came to accept that there are aspects of the world that will elude us. Some things will only get worse with increased effort, their capacity to absorb our ministrations infinite. But this does not mean we have given

E

up on perfection. Our scientists still try to concoct theories to explain the universe. Our writers still try to approach eternal truths. Our politicians even claim to want perfected government. But we no longer attempt to approach perfection directly, with brute force, as did Richardson. We pursue the asymptote with a sneaky reserve. Silence can be had through a surplus of words, success through failure, health through sickness.

In *Bartleby & Co.* Vila-Matas seems to argue in favour of a literature of silence. This is, of course, what the artists of no write. In contrast to them Vila-Matas gives us Camus, who is 'a yes-artist if ever there was one' because of 'his firm belief that art is the opposite of silence'. We could place Camus beside Richardson, because they see the world as something that can in theory be bounded, explained. Vila-Matas goes on to say that Camus, in the face of writers of silence like Beckett, 'would have been somewhat paralysed'. One imagines that Vila-Matas is correct here, that a writer of yes would have a hard time coming up with the words equal to a paradox like *expressing silence*, or, to a lesser degree, the cliché *the sound of silence*. These expressions are fundamentally ironic in nature, and thus potentially infinite. The challenge of revealing their infinity is clearly what motivates Vila-Matas, and, by extension, what I imagine ultimately motivated the great modernists of no. It seems ridiculous that anyone might seriously fault someone like Vila-Matas for failing to express silence, as Chabon seems to fault Joyce for failing to embody a dream. Mimesis is utterly beside the point for them. Attempting to express the clearly impossible-to-express frees them from its burden, tears away the crutches of realism so that they might crawl toward their asymptote. Or rather, it points the way toward a better mimesis: a mimesis of the internal, as opposed to the external. A mimesis that contradicts the very roots of the word, because a mimesis of the internal is a mimesis of what we can never see and feel but only intuit through experience, just as we can never actually see the structure of an atom but know it through inference and experimentation. A mimesis that floats atop the constructions given us by our great writers, a mimesis only consumable from within the accumulated myths of literary culture.

What exactly is meant by expressing silence? Beckett famously declared his ambition to 'drill one hole after another into the English language until that which lurks behind, be it something or nothing, starts seeping through'. This is a strange turn of phrase: how would 'nothing' seep through language? How would nothing do anything at all? That makes just about as much sense as drilling a hole into language with language. But the reason that Beckett is worthy of the highest regard is that his literature lived up to such statements with an authentic rigour and seriousness – and not with a mere pretention and the desire to shock. Vila-Matas attempts a similar kind of manoeuvre: he drills holes into the modernist consciousness by inscribing his work into it. BARTLEBY & CO. is a series of footnotes – actual footnotes lacking a source text – to the work of the great Bartlebys. Vila–Matas pries into his own personal canon by using their own words. Inspiration – which, tautologically, is the impulse to drill through the object of inspiration – always must come from somewhere. Harold Bloom claimed that his book THE ANXIETY OF INFLUENCE: A THEORY OF POETRY began with a nightmare that 'featured a covering cherub pressing down upon me'. In a sense, then, THE ANXIETY OF INFLUENCE is Bloom's attempt to represent one of his dreams in writing. No one would consider it a mimetic attempt, as Chabon does with Joyce; thus, Bloom's book cannot be impossible in the sense that the WAKE might be impossible. Bloom pursues a personal silence, Joyce pursues a collective one.

I speak to no one when I run, though I am surrounded by words I know by heart. It is a form of silent contemplation – the raps become a screen on which my thoughts may project. In no other aspect of life do I permit myself as much as an hour of pure, unpremeditated, unmediated thought. The closest would be reading, where, at its best, the written words become indistinguishable from my own thoughts. They become a way to think. When that happens, it becomes difficult to resist the urge to be drawn out of the book and begin to write. With running that is not an option. One cannot stop in the middle and pick up a pen. Inspiration comes not from words but from the euphoria of exertion. Thoughts are free to do what they will. They most frequently trace themselves into obsessive repetition. The same sentence drones, like a drum beat. It loops. It develops slight, insignificant variations. This is perhaps what thought, untrammelled, becomes when flush with its own inevitability, the capacity to exist according to its own ineluctable nature. By contrast, the friction of pushing these thoughts into words forces them into new shapes. They must seep into language in order to escape, like water finding the cracks and crevices of a glacier, taking on shapes unknown to human eyes. Perfection cannot be a mad dash toward infinity, a dash of articulation toward what is always possible. It can only come about on the perverse curve that denies direct approaches. Like light, thought is Apollonian. Light is truth, it defines our sight and orders our world. It nobly takes the shortest path between two points because it travels forward *without fail*. For us instead, light's children, words: the sacrifice, the ritual, the incantation, the drunkenness that gives a flash of insight.

The very best remedy I have for writer's block: reading. After scarcely a page of certain books I lose the ability to resist writing. The only way to continue would be to let the impulse abide. These books have become nearly impossible to read; many of them I have only read part way, feeling that I have gotten from them what I wanted.

E

We might also consider impossible literature as an attempt to exhaust a subject that is infinite, as all subjects are, or impossibly vast, as many subjects feel. In *INFINITE JEST* David Foster Wallace invents a film so fascinating that its viewers watch it unto death. They set the film on a repeating loop and sit there entranced, drooling, eventually dying of bodily neglect. It is infinite by means of repetition, like Beckett's play *PLAY*, which ends with the instruction that the actors are to repeat it. (It deals with a subject familiar to all but impossible to conclude: one man, two women.) This film is something of an artistic asymptote: the work of art so large that it can never be wholly consumed; rather, it consumes the viewer. The idea of recursion as a function of impossibility is important to Wallace's novel; addiction is the book's key sign, and the novel itself it has a loop-like structure, beginning at the temporal end and proceeding through to an ending that pushes readers back toward the physical beginning. This is meant to evoke the Ouroboros-like nature of desire, the impossibility that drives addiction from its absent centre, the self-reflexivity that underlies identity, language's failure to strike anything other than more language. These cycles produce a feeling of inevitability, a very modernistic sense of our inevitable failure: language *cannot* break free from itself, desire *cannot* be quenched. It is in playing with the notion of infinity as inevitable recursion that Wallace, like Vila-Matas, makes impossibility deeply human. Around this infinity collects the nodes of personhood. Our knowledge of failure is bound up with our knowledge of the infinite, of cycles, of the inevitable – these are the fundamental particles of our life. For Wallace, this understanding distinguishes human thought. And the capacity for literature to create its own in-finities is what lets a book break off from our world into its own. Trapped within a pit of language, the book becomes self-defining: we are not meant to leave the book's circuit, because its truth exists within it. This truth can only be expressed within the artefact of the book, but, somehow, the self-consuming snake Ouroboros bites us, even as its mouth remains trapped, choking on its own engorged tail.

A similar thing to *INFINITE JEST*'s recursion happens in Tom McCarthy's novel *REMAINDER*. The narrator pays actors to portray seemingly banal events in his life again, and again, and again, looping them indefinitely. These re-enactments occur in specific locations, made to look and feel like the place in which they originally occurred. One of them re-enacts a representative memory from the narrator's life when he was in early adulthood. He lived in an apartment building where he could smell the frying liver cooked by the lady living below him and the piano practice of the man living next to him. When I read this section of the novel it put me in mind of two apartments I had known: the apartment I lived in as a student at the University of California at Berkeley, and the apartment I rented for six months in Buenos Aires. I pictured McCarthy's narrator picturing some amalgam of those two thoughts of mine

E

as he attempted to construct an unalloyed memory.

As with Wallace and McCarthy, FINNEGANS WAKE deals obsessively with the idea of recursion. More than that: the book actually is a loop, with the final sentence continuing on back into the first. This is of a piece with modernism's asymptotic fantasy of representation: the gap between the page and the world is unbridgeable. They are both closed circles, not interlocking, not even touching. John Barth gets at this idea much more succinctly – in only ten words – in 'Frame-Tale', which reads in its entirety 'Once upon a time there was a story that began.' These words are printed top-to-bottom on the edge of the page, five to each side, and you are meant to cut the strip of paper out, twist it into a Möbius strip, and tape it shut so that it reads, 'Once upon a time there was a story that began Once upon a time there was a story that began Once upon a time there was a story that began…' Barth's tape expounds the relationship between literature, infinity, and time: it traces back into itself, incessantly beginning, unable to drive past a certain point and finding a story in that failure. As such, it is the skeleton of much larger works: what is TRISTRAM SHANDY but a grandiose version of this strip, festooned with so many more details? Barth's tape also reveals that what may appear straightforward to us – as Tristram Shandy's continual flight toward himself seems, from his perspective, a dash forward through the narration of his life – is actually a loop that brings us right back to where we started. So much of the impossible literature ends this way, cognisant of the cyclical nature of life and knowledge, having concluded that forward motion is not so desirable after all. It becomes clear that straightforward narration is not what interests these writers. They are more interested in the paradox that infinity can be understood but not explained.

The sign for infinity, of course, resembles a figure eight turned on its side. It looks a little like a track on which one might run, making as many circuits as one pleases, never getting anywhere but expending effort in the process. It has often occurred to me that I will never be able to predict when I will be done running. I, of course, picture myself running for all my life, ending up one of those somewhat distressingly gaunt, tautly muscled old men with wrinkled calves. In other words, I imagine it as infinite, as something that will survive within me until I expire. But that is just a projection of a boundless present into an unknown future. Like all things we imagine existing into perpetuity, like perpetuity itself, running is but a personal fantasy. Unlike literature, which can leave an impossible, infinite artefact, a little stone lodged in time, my own modest infinity must be powered by a continued desire to push it through to the next loop. The place this desire comes from, its nature is opaque to me. It is a part of myself that I perform, without knowledge of how or why. I only know the effects, which are ecstatic. There is truth and hope – even belief – in that feeling. A transitory truth, a belief that only lasts the hour that I sweat, but real nonetheless. In it I feel as though I am in the boundlessness of motion.

SPONSORS

TLS

THE TIMES LITERARY SUPPLEMENT

The leading international forum for literary culture

GRANTA

THE MAGAZINE OF NEW WRITING

'An indispensable part of the intellectual landscape'
– *Observer*

Every issue of *Granta* is a feast of the best new writing from
around the world. In our pages you'll find stories, reportage, poetry
and photography from the acclaimed and the infamous,
the prizewinners and the ones to watch.

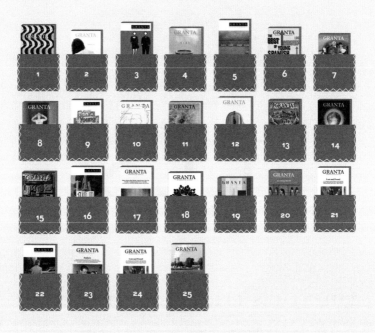

This Christmas, buy a gift subscription to *Granta*
and receive a 25% DISCOUNT. Four issues for just
£24 – that's a saving of £26 on the cover price.

Visit GRANTA.COM/WREV or call 0500 004 033

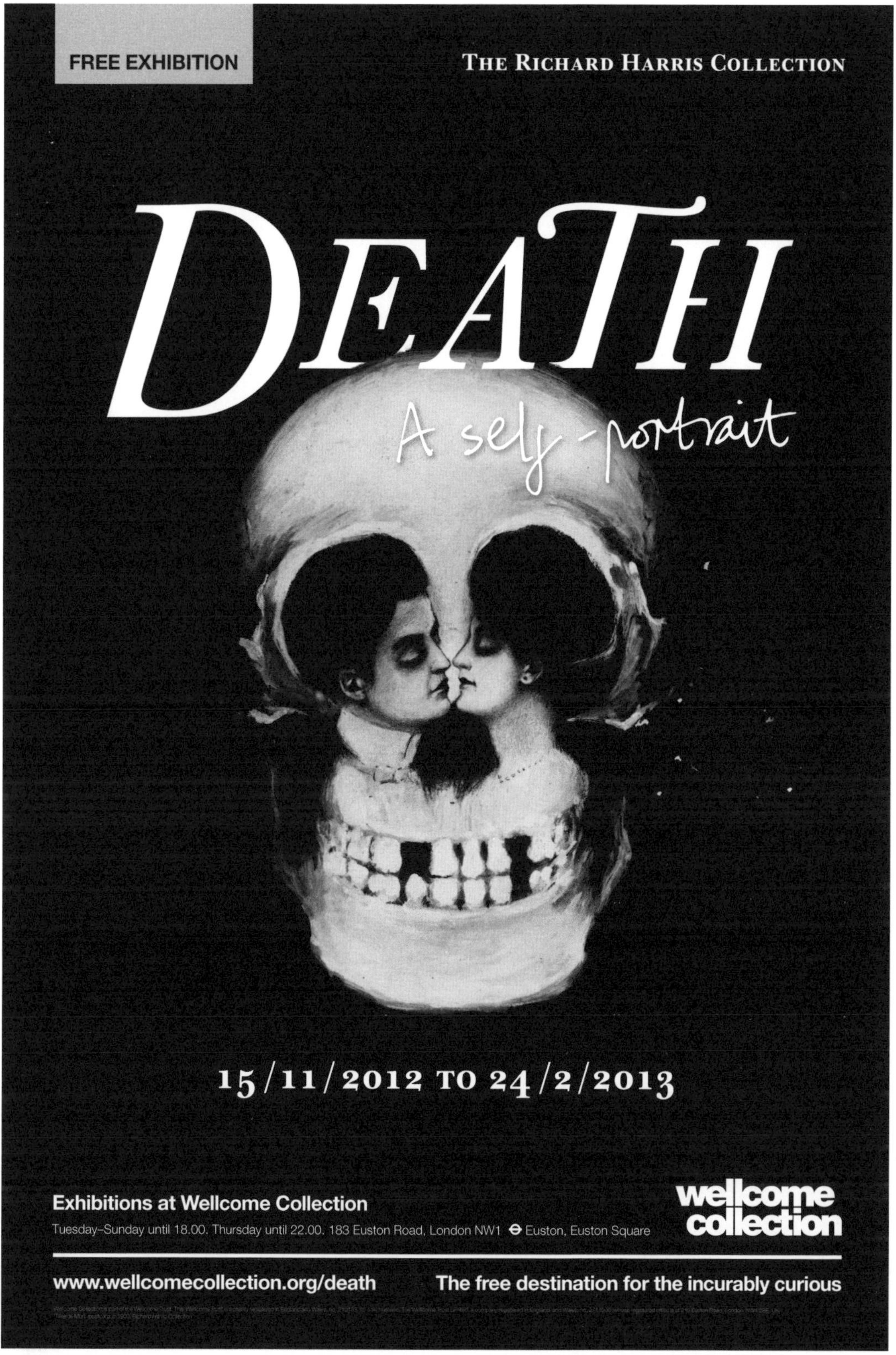
FREE EXHIBITION
THE RICHARD HARRIS COLLECTION
DEATH
A self-portrait
15/11/2012 TO 24/2/2013
Exhibitions at Wellcome Collection
Tuesday–Sunday until 18.00. Thursday until 22.00. 183 Euston Road, London NW1 Euston, Euston Square
wellcome collection
www.wellcomecollection.org/death
The free destination for the incurably curious

APPENDIX

CÉSAR AIRA is one of the most prolific writers in Argentina, having published more than eighty books to date. Besides essays and novels, Aira writes regularly for *EL PAÍS*. In 1996 he received a Guggenheim scholarship, and in 2002 he was shortlisted for the Rómulo Gallegos prize. In his 2003 novel *THE EAGLE'S THRONE*, Carlos Fuentes imagined that Aira had won the 2020 Nobel Prize.

EMILY BERRY's debut collection, *DEAR BOY*, will be published by Faber and Faber. She is a co-writer of *THE BREAKFAST BIBLE*, a forthcoming breakfast compendium.

JACOB BROMBERG is a poet, translator, and contributing editor to *THE WHITE REVIEW*. He lives in Paris, where he co-curates the Ivy Writers reading series.

MATT CONNORS is a painter. He lives and works in New York. Connors was awarded the John Simon Guggenheim Memorial Foundation Fellowship in 2012. His recent solo show at MoMA PS1 was his first museum presentation in the United States.

JACK COX was born and educated in Sydney. *DODGE ROSE*, a novel, will be published by Dalkey Archive Press next year.

HELEN DEWITT was born in Washington, DC but spent most of her childhood in South America. She was educated at Oxford University and has written two published novels, *THE LAST SAMURAI* and *LIGHTNING RODS*. DeWitt lives in Berlin.

SCOTT ESPOSITO is the author of *THE END OF OULIPO* (with Lauren Elkin), published by Zero Books. His writing has appeared in a number of leading newspapers and journals, and he edits *THE QUARTERLY CONVERSATION*, an online review of books and critical essays.

HUGH FOLEY is a writer and poet. His essays have been published in *REVIEW 31*. He lives in London.

EMMELINE FRANCIS is a contributing editor to *THE WHITE REVIEW*. She has worked in London and New York for Grove/Atlantic, Inc., *GRANTA* and Short Books.

SARAH HESKETH is a poet. She works as Events and Publications Manager for the Poetry Translation Centre.

OLIVIA MCCANNON's collection *EXACTLY MY OWN LENGTH* (Carcanet/Oxford Poets) was shortlisted for the Seamus Heaney Centre Prize, and won the 2012 Fenton Aldeburgh First Collection Prize.

ROSE MCLAREN lives in London and writes fiction, as well as travel pieces and articles on art, literature and film. She has written for various publications, including *CURIOCITY*, *THE JUNKET* and *THE WHITE REVIEW*.

DAN O'BRIEN is a poet and playwright based in Los Angeles.

KATHERINE SILVER is an award-winning literary translator and the co-director of the Banff International Literary Translation Centre (BILTC). Her most recent translations include works by Daniel Sada, César Aira, Horacio Castellanos Moya, Ernesto Mallo, and Carla Guelfenbein.

ERIK VAN DER WEIJDE resides in Brazil, having grown up in Holland, where he attended the Rijksakademie. Publishing under the moniker *4478ZINE*, his most recent publication *NIEMEYER* is the basis for his 2012 exhibition at Chert Gallery in Berlin.

GARTH WEISER graduated in 2005 from Columbia University in New York, where he currently lives and works. Weiser's paintings explore the nature of perception, using scale and perspective to disrupt visual expectations. Weiser's work has been shown at Casey Kaplan Gallery in New York and Altman Spiegel Gallery in San Francisco.

FRIENDS OF THE WHITE REVIEW

SALLY BAILEY

PIERS BARCLAY

ROSE BARCLAY

DAVID BARNETT

VALERIE BONNARDEL

JAMES BROOKES

SAM BROWN

ED BROWNE

ALBERT BUCHARD

MATHILDE CABANAS

THIBAULT CABANAS

CJ CAREY

NICOLAS CHAUVIN

KIERAN CLANCY

LEON DISCHE BECKER

CLAIRE DE DIVONNE

PHILIBERT DE DIVONNE

DAVID & BERNADETTE EASTHAM

HARRY ECCLES-WILLIAMS

MAX FARRAR

STEVE FLETCHER

HATTIE FOSTER

AUDE FOURGOUS

NATHAN FRANCIS

SKENDER GHILAGA

RICHARD GLUCKMAN

MATT GOLD

CYRILLE GONZALVES

MICHAEL GREENWOLD

ALEX GREINER

PATRICK HAMM

CAROL HUSTON

LEE JORDAN

JADE KOCH

LUISA DE LANCASTRE

CAROLINE LANGLEY

EUGENIA LAPTEVA

CAROLYN LEK

CHARLES LUTYENS

EMILY LUTYENS

ALEX MCDONALD

RUPERT MARTIN

SALLY MERCER

MINIMONIOTAKU

CYNTHIA & WILLIAM MORRISON-BELL

MARTIN NICHOLAS

VANESSA NICHOLAS

VITA PEACOCK

BEN POLLNER

PRIMORDIAL SEA

JORDAN RAZAVI

EDDIE REDMAYNE

GHISLAIN DE RINCQUESEN

DAVID ROSE

NICOLE SIBELET

SAMUEL NOAH SOLNICK

HENRIETTA SPIEGELBERG

ANASTASIA SVOBODA

GEORGETTE TESTARD

MARILOU TESTARD

PIERRE TESTARD

VERONIQUE TESTARD

MONICA TIMMS

MICHAEL TROUGHTON

WEFUND.CO.UK

SIMON WILLIAMS

JOHN WITNEY